HEARKEN

To The Spirit

THE FIGHT

Vol.2

Eva Bellamy

Published By: Tel A Vision Publishing, LLC

Copyright © 2023 by Secretarial State

Copyright © 2023 by Eva Bellamy

ISBN 978-0-9794065-5-3

Library of Congress Number: 2017909565

Cover Design: Rebecacovers

Typography: Tel A Vision Publishing

Copyediting: Sarah T.

Printed in the U.S.A.

SPECIAL THANKS

To My Lord and Savior, Jesus Christ; thank you so much for making intercession for me to Our Father in Heaven. He has strengthened me to continue on this journey, writing the sequels to "The Spirit Has Spoken." We have completed sequel #2, with one more to go. It is you who started has begun a great work in me, and Father, I thank you for finishing it. I bless your Holy Name.

Table of Contents

ACKNOWLEDGMENTS

A special acknowledgment goes to my Mother, Dorothy Bellamy, as she rests in peace. Thank you for all your love. You'll always be in my heart. I Love You.

Special thanks to my two beautiful children, Kendra and Kamrin. You both are my delight and inspiration. Mommy knows that it hasn't been easy for us, but you all have encouraged me over the years with your support, long-suffering and perseverance. I love you both so much.

For the many that have impacted my life in a tremendous way, thank you so much. You've played a huge part in helping me fulfill the plan of the Lord.

INTRODUCTION

The Spirit Has Spoken (Volume 1) revealed Evie's story, but didn't reveal the mystery of her parents. In this book, The Spirit Has Spoken Again (Volume 2), we begin to see Evie's journey of living out her salvation. She hasn't yet taken seriously the importance of what it means to be saved. In the same way that God has a plan for her life, Satan has a plan as well and will continue to have one until the return of Christ.

Evie goes through straddling the fence because of an un-renewed mind. Eventually, she'll realize that she has to walk out her salvation with fear and trembling. John 10:10 (KJV) says, "The thief cometh not, but for to steal, and to kill, and to destroy. I am come that they might have life, and that they might have it more abundantly." Satan tries to strike at her once again. Will Evie live the abundant life Christ promised?

God continues to speak and to lead Evie and Satan does the same. Different voices insist on trying to control her destiny, but whose voice will she obey?   Will she learn how to forgive and let go of her past? The mystery of what happened to her family remains while her long lost best friend, Torri, wants to help. Will she let her in? Let's hear what the Spirit of God has to say.

CHAPTER ONE
A New Beginning

Daylight shone through the windows of the Kleins' home. Birds chirped from outdoors. Bishop Kenneth Klein sat at the kitchen table reading the newspaper. He picked up his glass of orange juice. Mrs. Klein strutted into the kitchen in a classic beige suit and red heels. She moved toward the stove, and removed a pot, turning off the knob. Bishop stared at his wife with a grin while drinking his orange juice. Deborah opened the kitchen drawer, taking out a blue apron and tying it around her waist.

"Baby, do you need my help?" Bishop put down his glass, looking at his wife. He stood and walked toward her.

"You can grab the plates," Deborah him. Kenneth looked over his shoulder, slipping a piece of bacon from the bowl and crunching it into his mouth. "I saw that," Deborah glared at him while she walked to the stove. Continuing to give her husband a sharp eye, she grabbed the glass bowl of bacon and placed it on the table. Meanwhile, the Bishop walked to the kitchen table, putting the plates on the placemats. Evie entered the room.

"Well, good morning!" Mrs. Klein turned around, greeting Evie with a smile. Evie walked to the kitchen table and sat down. "How did you sleep?" Bishop Klein asked as he walked to the counter, grabbing the bowl of cheese eggs and the basket of homemade biscuits.

"Alright, I guess," Evie answered hopelessly. Bishop Klein looked at Evie's troubled presence, "Let's eat!" Mrs. Klein took her seat. They joined hands and Deborah looked at her husband.

The Bishop's deep voice resonated throughout the room, "Heavenly Father, we come before you on this day that you have made. God, we ask that you bless this food and the hands which prepared it. In Jesus' name we pray. Amen?"

"Amen," Evie and Mrs. Klein agreed.

Evie dug into the cheese eggs bowl, placing a large spoonful on her plate. Quietly, she took a biscuit, and then several strips of bacon. Bishop and Mrs. Klein looked at one another.

"Evie, are you excited about your first day of a new beginning?" Bishop Klein asked, chewing.

No response. Evie sipped her orange juice. Deborah Klein glanced Evie's way, "Evie is there something wrong?"

Evie took a strong swallow, placing her glass down. Picking up a strip of bacon from her plate, she ate, staring at the Kleins.

"Yes, there is something wrong!" Evie answered sarcastically. "My life has been hell, yet you sit at this table and pretend like everything is alright. My parents… only God knows where they are. I've been living in turmoil since I was eight. I'm nineteen, in a house with two strangers, and I don't know what to expect! You both could be killers in a clergy collar far as I can see. My grandparents were pastors and my grandmother was mean as a snake disguised in old weave." Mrs. Klein grinned at Evie's figure of speech.

"So how can you help me when I don't trust you? Look at me! I am motherless, I am fatherless. The only parents I had deserted me."

"There is hope, Evie," Bishop responded, reaching over and grabbing his Bible from the edge of the center counter.

"According to the word of God, Evie, it says in Psalms 27:10, **'When my father and my mother forsake me, then the LORD will take me up**.' God has taken you up as His very own daughter!" Mrs. Klein looked at Evie as her face lit up to Bishop's words. He continued.

"You see, God is a mother to the motherless and a father to the fatherless. The book of Isaiah 49:15 says, **'Can a mother forget the baby at her breast and have no compassion on the child she has borne? Though she may forget, I will not forget you!'**

Although it appears as though you've been forsaken, God has not forgotten about you. Mrs. Klein and I may not be your biological parents, but we are the spiritual parents you need in this season of your life. Only God knows the truth regarding your parents. He wants to reveal himself to you, Evie."

"I guess." Evie shook her head. "Okay, so what about all of the people who are after me?" Deborah sighed and looked at her husband, reaching for the Bible. He handed it to her.

"Evie, read verses one through nine in Psalms chapter 27, and those scriptures will answer your question." Evie looked at her, then took the Bible and read,

"The LORD is my light and my salvation; whom shall I fear? The LORD is the strength of my life; of whom shall I be afraid? When the wicked, even my enemies and my foes, came upon me to eat up my flesh, they stumbled and fell. Though an host should encamp against me, my heart shall not fear: though war should

rise against me, in this will I be confident. One thing have I desired of the LORD, that will I seek after; that I may dwell in the house of the LORD all the days of my life, to behold the beauty of the LORD, and to inquire in his temple. For in the time of trouble he shall hide me in his pavilion: in the secret of his tabernacle shall he hide me; he shall set me up on a rock. And now shall my head be lifted up above my enemies round about me: therefore will I offer in his tabernacle sacrifices of joy; I will sing, yes, I will sing praises to the LORD. Hear, O LORD, when I cry with my voice: have mercy also on me, and answer me. When you said, Seek you my face; my heart said to you, your face, LORD, will I seek. Hide not your face far from me; put not your servant away in anger: you have been my help; leave me not, neither forsake me, O God of my salvation."

Evie looked up at Mrs. Klein.

"In other words, God is our guiding light through our walk of salvation. With Him being our protector, we shall not fear what man may do to us. Fear is a dark shadow that envelops us and ultimately imprisons us. But God is the strong tower of our lives, and in Him you shall not see darkness. Even if your enemy tries to come against you, no weapon formed against you shall prosper. They may speak things against you that may cringe your flesh; God will cause them to stumble in their tracks. As you remain in the Lord, you will not fear. And the more you remain in Him, Evie, you will desire the Lord more and more. When trouble tries to rise up against you, He will cover you. Your enemies will no longer see you. He'll hide you! God will teach you to live in His presence, and from that, you will learn his gentle touch as a parent."

Mrs. Klein smiled at Evie compassionately, her pearly white teeth radiating the room.

Bishop looked at his watch. He stood, "Honey, I have to get going. I'll meet you at school." He kissed his wife.

"Evie, God has great plans for you and it's no coincidence you're here. We are here to love you as Christ would have us to and to shepherd you as Jesus instructed. Moreover, we are here to guide you to the abundant life God has chosen for you, Amen! With that said, we welcome you into this house! This is your new home, and we love you." Bishop smiled with open arms. Evie stood and hesitantly embraced Bishop Klein.

Deborah smiled. Bishop kissed Evie on the forehead and then kissed her on the cheek. Deborah experienced a flashback: "Remember, Daddy loves you," Kenneth kissing Shelia on the forehead.

Bishop Klein stared at his wife with a pause. He smiled and kissed her on the side of her cheek. "Baby, you okay?" Deborah snapped out of her day dream. "Y-yes, I'm okay," she stuttered. "I love you." Bishop regarded her with a smile. "I love you, too," he said as he left the room.

Refocusing her attention on Evie, Mrs. Klein stretched across the kitchen table and grabbed both of Evie's hands.

"I know that you have many questions concerning your parents. Petition them to the Lord, Evie. God wants to commune and talk with you. And I promise, if you just open up your heart and let him in, He will reveal many things to you. Matthew 6:33 says, **"Seek ye first the kingdom of God, and His righteousness; and all these things shall be added unto you."** If you seek God with everything within you, answers will be given to you. Okay?"

Evie nodded her head. Mrs. Klein stood up from the table. She reached over and kissed Evie on the forehead. Evie closed her eyes. She looked up again and saw her mother's face instead of Mrs. Klein's. Evie made a puzzled face.

"Evie, are you okay?" Mrs. Klein asked. Evie closed her eyes and reopened them, now seeing Mrs. Klein staring back at her.

"I'm okay," Evie answered.

"Well, we have to get going." She grabbed the bacon and biscuit bowls, walked to the stove and placed them inside the oven.

"Evie, do you mind giving me a hand? You can clear off the table." Mrs. Klein smiled.

"Sure." Evie stood; gathering the plates.

"When you're done, I'll meet you in the car." Mrs. Klein instructed and left the kitchen. Evie walked over to the kitchen sink.

"Do you see that knife? Pick it up and slice your wrist. They don't love you." An evil voice spoke to Evie. Evie placed her hands over her ears and walked away from the sink, back to the kitchen table.

"Shut up!" Evie screamed, grabbing the pitcher of orange juice and stacked glasses. Walking back to the sink, she set the orange juice on the counter while gently placing the glasses in the sink.

"They're going to kill you first if you don't." She grabbed the orange juice container and put it into the refrigerator.

"They are pretending to like you. Go ahead and run away," the voice continued to torment her. Evie pressed her hands to her ears.

"NO! Stop it! Stop talking to me. No! Shut up! Stop it!" Evie screamed in rage. Mrs. Klein rushed in and grabbed Evie's arms.

"I speak to you Satan right now in the Mighty name of Jesus! Loose your stronghold off of Evie Young, right now, in the name of Jesus! We rebuke you, and we command you to get under her feet in the name of Jesus! We release from Heaven a sound mind. Peace, I speak." Evie cried at the sound of Mrs. Klein's rebuke.

"It's okay, Evie," Deborah assured her.

"I keep hearing this voice that's telling me to kill myself and that you two don't love me."

"Evie, Satan is plotting to turn you against yourself. Do not entertain those evil voices. When you hear them, tell Satan that you rebuke him in the name of Jesus and you command him to get under your feet." She held Evie tightly.

"You're fine. Go upstairs and get your shoes so we can go." Evie went upstairs.

Deborah sighed, placing her right hand on her hip. **"Daughter, you must begin to teach Evie how to work out her salvation with fear and trembling. Teach her how to hear My voice and to stand against the wiles of the devil, so that she may be able to stand,"** the Spirit of God spoke to Deborah Klein. Evie returned to the kitchen in her black boots with her purse on her shoulder.

"Alright, let's go." Mrs. Klein walked ahead to the garage entrance. Evie followed.

Bishop Klein stood at the file cabinet in his office; a blonde Caucasian woman entered with a folder in her hand.

"Bishop, Evie Young's transcript came in." He retrieved it.

"Thank you, April," Bishop smiled. He closed the file cabinet and walked over to his desk. Taking a seat, he stared at a family picture of Deborah, his daughter and himself. The thought of Shelia weighed on his mind, bringing flashbacks of the funeral. He touched his daughter's face. He placed the picture down, picked up the phone on his desk and dialed.

"Deborah, where are you?" Bishop leaned back in his black leather chair. He turned it toward the window, looking out at all of Atlanta.

"We are about three minutes away." Deborah glanced over at Evie on the passenger side. Evie looked sad.

"Okay dear, we'll see you shortly." Deborah clicked off the car's Bluetooth. She turned the corner. Evie stared at a homeless woman sitting on a bench. Turning into the parking lot of Kings and Queens of Faith University, Mrs. Klein glanced over at Evie.

"Evie, I know what you are feeling."

"You think you do?" Evie responded sarcastically. Mrs. Klein sighed.

"Your life has been a journey. But you must believe that God has an unexpected end for you," she said, glancing at Evie.

"My parents have been missing almost eleven years now. There is a voice constantly telling me to give up on life. Then there is another voice that says 'Don't give up hope, Evie.'"

"You listen to the good voice that overpowers the negative." Mrs. Klein smiled.

"God has a perfect plan for your life and I promise you, out of all the things you've tried in your life; this time truly trust Christ and watch and see what He does for you. Amen?" Mrs. Klein pulled into the parking space, placing the gear in park. The car jerked to a final stop.

"I guess," Evie responded inattentively. Mrs. Klein grinned and opened the driver's door.

"Come on, let's get you registered." Mrs. Klein set her feet on the pavement and stood, closing the door. Evie slothfully got out of the car then slammed the door. They walked toward the campus. Viewing the clear blue sky, Evie lifted her head high, staring into the sunlight. The strength of the light beamed radiantly, causing her to blink. She looked ahead. Walking up two flights of stairs, they entered the building.

"Good morning, Prophetess Klein."

"Good morning, Corey, how are you doing today?" She greets him with a smile.

"I am blessed and I bless God that I am here," Corey replied, looking at Evie.

"Amen! Corey, this is Evie Young, our spiritual daughter. She'll be attending classes here."

"Amen! Nice to meet you, Evie. I am Corey, school security. If you ever need anything while I'm in the hallway, don't hesitate to ask."

"Thanks," Evie responded without interest. Mrs. Klein looked at Evie's expression.

"Well, we better get upstairs and get Evie situated for class." Corey grinned; both ladies made their way up the swirled marble double staircase. Evie looked up at the crystal chandelier; they reached the top of the stairs. Other students passed by in the hallway as Evie and Mrs. Klein walked across the foot traffic and into the office. Evie looked at the principal's nameplate on the front door.

Walking past the secretary's desk, they entered into Bishop Klein's office. He looked up and then looked at his watch.

"Perfect timing! Have a seat, Evie." Mrs. Klein walked over to her desk. Bishop pulled papers out of the folder.

"Your transcripts came in, and I was reviewing them. I do have some questions. Now, it says here that you were a senior and you received credit for the first quarter, but for the last quarter, they did not credit you. Is there a reason why?" Evie sat in angry silence. Mrs. Klein glanced at her.

"Kenneth, I mentioned to you that Evie dropped out her senior year." Bishop Klein remembered and started to speak.

"Yes, I dropped out," Evie replied with such passion in her voice that Bishop Klein looked up. "Let me guess, your next question is why, so let me answer that for you. Once in my life, I cherished education, life, and the expectation of going to college. Ask me, do I care now?"

Bishop nodded his head for Evie to proceed. "Do you care, Evie? About the life God has for you in spite of what has happened in the past?"

Evie looked at Mrs. Klein and Bishop quietly, while scratching her head through her curly hair. "How do I know God is real? Honestly, I don't believe he is. So what, I was raised in church! And yes, I have family who says that they're Christians. But if God is love and if he is such a great God, why in the hell did he allow me to be molested? Why did he allow me to be raped continually? And why did he take my parents away from me? Answer that for me, please, Mr. Bishop and Mrs. Prophetess!" Bishop and his wife stared quietly at each other.

"Evie, as believers, there are so many trials and tribulations we all go through for the sake of Christ. Begin to study the book of Peter, and you'll learn that when someone goes through adversity in their lives, it doesn't mean that God has turned his back on them. And sometimes we pay the price of sin because of another person's disobedience. But at the end of it all, there's a blessing for every test and a penalty for every sin."

"So, basically what you are telling me is, I went through all the things I've been through because of my parents' sin?" Evie looked ready to fight. Mrs. Klein stood up from her desk and walked over, sitting on the edge of Bishop Klein's desk.

"Evie, what Bishop means is, we all were once sinners, saved by grace through Christ Jesus. Once He saves us from sin and death, we still fall short of his glory. Although our ancestors may have passed on sin through the blood line, each and every individual who confesses Jesus as Lord has a choice to become redeemed from that curse. In Matthew 16:24, Jesus tells his disciples to deny themselves, pick up their crosses and follow him. There are going to be things in life that will become heavy upon you when walking this walk. But that is when we have to surrender our burdens to the Lord, casting our cares upon him. He cares for you, Evie."

Mrs. Klein leaned over toward her. "We are not going to focus on what has happened in the past, or where your parents are. We are going to focus on Evie getting to know Jesus for herself. And by you doing that, the Spirit of the Lord will give you answers to the mystery of your parents."

Bishop Klein gazed at his wife as she continued, "We are not going to focus on why you dropped out. This is a new season. Our mission is to see to it that you are walking in the fullness of God's purpose and plan for your life. So, the first step is helping you finish out your senior year. Amen!" Mrs. Klein stood up, and she walked over to the walkie-talkie on her desk.

Evie rolled her eyes.

The static of the walkie-talkie broke the silence. "Cory, come in."

"Here. Over," Cory responded.

"Cory, can you get one of the officers to cover your post? We need you immediately in our office."

"10-4," Cory replied. Mrs. Klein replaced the walkie-talkie on her desk. The Bishop typed numbers into the computer. Mrs. Klein wrote information on a form.

Cory walked in. "What can I do for you, Bishop and Prophetess?" Cory inquired. Mrs. Klein put the black ink pen down and walked over to Cory.

"Cory, can you please walk Evie over to the G-wing, room 1024? She needs to take a placement test."

"Sure."

"Give this form to Professor Joseph and he'll take it from there."

"Evie, you're going to take an evaluation test so we can finalize your schedule. The test is about an hour and forty-five minutes. Cory is going to escort you there, then to lunch, and then back to our office. Do you have any questions?" Mrs. Klein looked at Evie. She glared back in anger. Mrs. Klein looked over at Bishop; their eyes met. Evie stood silently and walked out of the office. Cory cracked a smile and followed Evie.

"Thanks, Cory."

"Not a problem. Let me know if there's anything else I can help you with." Cory responded. Mrs. Klein walked toward the oak office door and shut it gently as the two leave. Bishop Klein stopped typing, leaning back in his chair. He looked at his wife. She sat down in the chair in front of his desk.

"I apologize, dear, if I overstepped my position as a wife, but I saw that a spirit that was trying to wrestle with you. And as a spiritual mother, I had to shut down all of the confusion. God is not the author of it. We will not baby her, but we will train her up to be an ambassador of Christ." Bishop smiled.

"Baby you're fine. No apology needed. I know the Lord was using you. I know Evie is wounded, but God is a healer and she's going to make it. Amen." Bishop stood and walked toward his wife. She stood up and he kissed her lips.

"Amen." Deborah smiled.

"I have a 10 o'clock meeting with one of the Bishops for the convention. Do you need anything before I go?"

"No, honey, I'm fine." She walked her husband to the door.

"Okay, well, I'll be back around 2 o'clock. I love you."

"I love you too, dear." Bishop left and Mrs. Klein closed the door. She walked back to her desk and with an exhale lifted her hands toward the ceiling.

"Lord, I bless your name! Father, I ask you to strengthen me on this day, O God. I ask you, Lord, to keep me in your will and if I've sinned toward you by being out of order with Evie, Lord please forgive me. Father, continue to help me to be a leader by your Spirit and not of myself. Lord, I ask you to continue to heal Evie and deliver her from all unrighteousness. Raise her up to be the woman of God you've called her to be, Father. Teach her your voice so that a voice of a stranger she shall and will not follow. Continue to send her other people to help raise her up in the things of you, Lord. I bless your Holy name and thank you in advance for hearing this prayer. In Jesus' name I pray, Amen."

CHAPTER TWO

The Fight

Students flooded the hallway. As Cory and Evie navigated through the traffic, Evie spotted a long-lost friend. Torri rushed over, but Evie continued to walk with Cory toward the elevator. Cory pressed the button. Torri walked up to Evie, her hands full of books.

"Evie, it's so good to see you again!" Torri greeted her. Ruth, Torri's class-mate, approached.

"Too bad I can't say the same," Evie snapped, then glared at Ruth. The elevator door opened. Evie and Cory stepped in. He pressed the basement floor button. Evie faced forward, ignoring Torri's puzzled expression as the doors close.

"You know Torri?" Cory asked.

"Unfortunately," Evie responded as the elevator opened.

"What is that supposed to mean?" Cory asked as they exited the elevator, turned the corner and walked down the hallway.

"Torri is a long lost "friend" I wish I'd never met. Can we drop the subject now?" Evie's brown eyes enlarged meaningfully. Cory cracked a dry smile as they approached their destination. He opened the door for Evie.

"Today, class, we are going to learn about different types of inner voices. Psychologists say that if a person hears inner voices, they are hallucinating. I began to research the word 'hallucination,' and it was interesting," Minister Klein II taught his class. Torri folded her arms and continued to listen. Minister Klein sat on the edge of his desk and grabbed a sheet a paper from a stack.

"I printed these out because I wanted to share this information with you all." Minister Klein II gave the stack to the first row. The students passed the papers back.

The students started reading as Minister Klein continued, "An auditory hallucination is a form of hallucination that involves perceiving sound without auditory stimulus. A common form involves hearing one or more voices. This may be associated with psychotic disorders such as schizophrenia or mania, and holds special significance in diagnosing these conditions. There are three main categories in which these conditions can fall: a person hearing a voice speaking one's thoughts, a person hearing one or more voices arguing, or a person hearing a voice narrating his or her own actions. However, individuals may hear voices without suffering from diagnosable mental illness. The 'Hearing Voices Movement,' is a support and advocacy group for people who hear voices, but do not otherwise show signs of mental illness or impairment." Minister Klein II looked up from the paper to his students. He continued to read.

"Other types of auditory hallucination include exploding head syndrome and musical ear syndrome. In the latter, people will hear music playing in their mind, usually songs they are familiar with. Recent reports have also mentioned that it is also possible to get musical hallucinations from listening to music for long periods of time. This condition can be caused by lesions on the brain stem (often resulting from a stroke); also, tumors, encephalitis, or abscesses. Other reasons include hearing loss and epileptic activity." Minister Klein II looked at the students as some hands go up.

"Before I answer any questions, I would like you to take a 'Selah' moment. Let that marinate. What I just read is a summary of the assumptions of psychiatry. These scientists did not create nor make mankind or the earth. All they do is try to perceive and then give predictions of how people may behave. When people take God out of the equation, the world will always have difficulty knowing the truth. John, you have a question?"

"Yes, I remember when I smoked weed. There were times I heard voices saying, 'Don't smoke that.' Then another voice telling me, 'Man, smoke that joint, and when you get done go call your boys and rob a gas station.' One day my grandmother who was an Evangelist told me that it was the Holy Spirit speaking, telling me not to smoke. She showed me the scriptures, I believe it's 1 Corinthians 6:19-20, "Do you not know that your body is the temple of the Holy Spirit, who is in you, whom you have received from God. You are not your own." Then she said it was Satan telling me to go steal. The Bible says, "You shall not steal." Satan, who is evil, will always try to go against God, who is good. But although I know my Bible, I struggle with them voices; I'm not going to lie." Minister Klein II walked over to the dry erase board.

"John, thank you for sharing that. Everyone put your hands down for a moment. We'll continue with questions and answers in a minute. First, I want you all to write down some notes that I believe will answer most of your questions." He wrote on the whiteboard as some students took notes; others were looking for something to write with. Minister Klein continued to write on the whiteboard until he was finished. He put down the marker.

"We are going to take a look at Genesis chapter one, verse twenty-six. It reads like this." Minister Klein looked up and saw students looking for pens and paper.

"For those who are with me, please help those who are still scrambling for something to write with." Isaiah looked into his pencil case. Smiling at Torri, he gave her a pen.

"Okay, Genesis 1:26 says, (KJV) **"And God said, Let us make man in our image, after our likeness; and let them have dominion over the fish of the sea, and over the fowl of the air, and over the cattle, and over all the**

earth, and over every creeping thing that creepeth upon the earth," Minister Klein read.

"Do you notice in this passage, it says, God created us? There are some words I want you to write down." He pointed to the whiteboard.

"'God said, Let Us make.' These five words are the foundation of who you are. You are the product of God's actions! Can someone tell me who is the 'Us' that God is referring to? Torri?"

"God the Father, God the Son, and God the Holy Spirit."

"Very good! Can someone tell me who these three are?" Minister Klein waits to call on another student. All hands remain down.

"Isaiah."

He stood up. "God the Father, God the Son and God the Holy Spirit are the three persons of the Trinity of the Godhead that is equivalent to one. The word "Godhead" occurs three times in the scriptures Acts 17:29, Romans 1:20, and Colossians 2:9." Isaiah walked toward the front of the class as he continues.

"There are two different Greek words translated 'Godhead': *theiotes* and *theotes*. Thayer says Godhead (**theiotes**) means, 'divinity and divine nature'[1]. The difference between these two words is that *theiotes* has to do with the attributes of God, His Divine nature, and properties. *Theotes* indicates the Divine essence of the Godhead; the personality of God. [2] The Godhead, then, is divinity, divine nature, and the essence of God, simply stated. It is essential that we also understand the term that inspired writers used to designate the Creator: 'God.' God

---

[1]Thayer, Joseph H. Thayer's Greek-English Lexicon, pg. 285.

[2] W. E. Vine, Expository Dictionary of New Testament Words.

is from the Greek '*theios,*' which means 'divine, deity.'[3]" Isaiah stood next to Minister Klein with a smile.

"Class, give Mr. Scholar Isaiah Wade a hand clap," Minister Klein insisted. The class gave Isaiah a standing ovation.

"Very impressive, Isaiah. Would you like to teach the class?"

"I'm not that impressive." The class laughed. He walked back to his desk and sat down. Minister Klein looked at the clock on the wall.

"We are out of time for today, but we will pick back up where we left off. Homework! I would like everyone to finish writing the information from the board. Read and meditate on Genesis 1:26, Jeremiah 1:5, Hebrews 1:1 and Isaiah 64:8. In your own words, I would like you to

---

[3] Thayer, pg. 285.

answer: 'Why did God come down in the form of flesh to save us?' Any further questions?" Minister Klein asked the class.

"Yes, I have a question. Does God speak to sinners?" Ruth asked.

"That is an excellent question. By the end of the week, we are going to touch on that. In the meanwhile, study your Bibles, everyone; don't just read them. There is a huge difference."

Minister Klein walked to his desk and took a seat while the class prepared for dismissal. Torri walked up to her teacher's desk. Minister Klein looked up from writing.

"Yes, Torri?"

"Minister Klein, can I speak with you for a moment?"

"Sure." The bell rang. The students began clearing the classroom. Isaiah and Torri smiled at one another. Minister Klein stood up.

"One minute, Torri. Everyone enjoy the rest of your day and see you bright and early tomorrow!"

"You, too," some of the students responded. Minister Klein walked behind the last student and closed the door. He walked back to his desk. Torri took a seat in the front row.

"What's on your mind, Torri?"

"Say you have a friend that you've known practically all your life. And then all of the sudden you lose contact with them. Ten years later, God not only brings them back into your life, but they return with scars."

"Okay." Minister Klein nodded, waiting for Torri to finish.

"And say that you've tried everything you can possibly think of, but they insist on blaming you for their pain. What would you do?"

"Well... first thing, Torri, is that you have to continue to pray for your friend. Secondly, the Spirit of God is telling me that your friend is battling with different voices speaking in their mind. They are very confused and we both know that Satan is the author of confusion." Torri nodded her head at Minister Klein.

"They also have anger toward God. There are some things that have happened in your friends' life that they blame God for. But you and I know that God is a loving and a caring God. Stay in fervent prayer for them. Pray that Christ enters in and opens up their heart because it is very hardened right now. Also, pray that the true love of God embraces and penetrates their very being. When people are blinded from wounds, they cannot see the truth. So, I agree with you, right now, in the name of Jesus that your friend's eyes of understanding will be opened to the truth." Minister Klein stood with Torri. She walked over to his desk.

"Thanks, Minister Klein." Torri showed her appreciation by shaking her teacher's hand.

"Anytime, Torri. Well, I have to prepare for my next class." Minister Klein walked over to the door. Torri grabbed her belongings and walked to the door. He opened it as other students began to enter the classroom.

"See you tomorrow," she smiled.

"Okay Torri, enjoy the rest of your day." He walked over to the white board and erased what he had written there.

Isaiah jumped out from the right of Torri as she left Minister Klein's class. Their lips touched.

"You waited for me? Aww, isn't that sweet?" Torri smiled at Isaiah. He took her books and carried them as they walked down the hall.

"Thanks, Mr. Scholar. Someone was showing off today!"

"No show-off here. I felt like being deep and spiritual, my queen." Isaiah smiled with a laugh. Torri laughed and blushed. They continued to walk down the hallway, turning the corner.

"So what did you and Minister Klein talk about?"

"About Evie. I was excited to see her today. And as usual, I am not one of her favorites. Minister Klein pretty much told me to just pray for her."

"Hmm, sounds familiar." Torri stopped at the door of her next class and playfully hit Isaiah on his arm. The bell rang.

"Give me my books." Torri smiled at Isaiah, snatching her books from him. He kissed her on the cheek.

"See you later." Torri entered into her classroom. Isaiah ran down the hall to his.

Evie looked up from finishing her test. She looked around at the other students that were testing and placed the scantron into her test booklet. Standing, she walked to the front and handed the test booklet to the instructor.

"Thank you. You have another forty minutes in this class. You can either stay here until next period, or I can write you a pass back to the Klein's office," Professor Joseph whispered. "You can wait there until next period."

"Yeah, that's fine. Where is the rest room?" Evie asked.

"When you go out that door, make a left, straight down the hall on your right." Professor Joseph scribbled a hall pass and handed it to Evie.

"Thanks." Evie clutched it, walked toward the back of the classroom and found her way to the rest room.

"You don't have to go to the bathroom. Hold it and leave. You don't need school. You flunked the test anyway. You're dumb. You never were anything and you will never be anything. Leave! You don't fit in anyway."

Evie placed her hands over her ears. The voice continued. She ran into the bathroom.

Mrs. Klein finished her conversation with the secretary.

"Thanks, April."

"You're welcome, Prophetess Klein." April went back to her desk while Mrs. Klein left the office. She walked down the hall, entering the main office where the administration personnel sat.

"Good morning, Prophetess Klein."

"Good morning, ladies." Passing their desks and into the Vice Principle's office, she knocked on the open door.

"Good morning, Mrs. Santos."

"Good morning, Mrs. Klein, please have a seat." The ladies greeted each other with a hug, and Mrs. Klein took a seat in front of Mrs. Santo's desk.

"Professor Joseph scanned and emailed Evie's test. We're waiting now for it to process through the system. The scores should be available shortly. In the meanwhile, we have a preliminary schedule for the remaining of this semester. Of course, it's subject to change depending on her test scores. If she scores well, she will be able to graduate in May. If not, she will graduate, but not until December." Mrs. Santos advised.

"Certainly," Mrs. Klein agreed. Mrs. Santos' computer beeped.

"Let's see, I believe her test scores are in." Her red finger nail relaxed on the black mouse. She clicked, and then typed, pressing enter to send. She gazed at the screen.

"Unbelievable!" Mrs. Santo she stared at the screen then turned her monitor around for Mrs. Klein to see.

"A 4.0? Bless the Lord!" Mrs. Klein smiled.

"You have a smart cookie! According to her transcript and her placement test, this qualifies her to graduate this year!" She handed Evie's schedule over.

"Thank you, Mrs. Santos." Mrs. Klein stood, holding the schedule.

"My pleasure! Let me know if you need anything else."

"I will." Mrs. Klein smiled, leaving Mrs. Santos' office. Grabbing her walkie-talkie from her hip. As she walked back through the administrative office, she brought it to her face.

"Cory, pick up."

"This is Cory, go ahead."

"Can you bring Evie back to my office, please?"

"Yes, ma'am."

"Thanks."

"10/4," Cory made an about face and entered the testing room.

"Professor Joseph, where is Evie?"

"I wrote her a pass 15 minutes ago to Bishop and Prophetess Klein's office."

"Thank you." Cory left quickly.

"Mrs. Klein, come in." He spoke on his receiver.

"Yes, Cory," Mrs. Klein responded, Cory walked down the hallway.

"Professor Joseph said he dismissed Evie back to your office about 15 minutes ago."

"Fifteen minutes ago? She should've been here by now. I hope she didn't get lost. Did you tell him you were going to return to escort her back to me?"

"Yes, I did. But we are talking about 72-year-old man." Cory walked back to the security stand. The bell rang.

"Once the halls clear out, if she hasn't made it back to the office, I'll see if I can find her. I know she's around her somewhere." Cory sat down at his desk and looked at the students through the security monitor.

"Okay," Mrs. Klein responded unsurely, walking toward her office. She turned the volume down to her radio.

"Lord, I don't like this feeling I am getting in my spirit."
Mrs. Klein walked into her office and shut the door.

CHAPTER THREE

He's Back

As Evie ran away from the school, she looked both ways crossing the street. Stopping by a bench in a park, she tried to catch her breath, both hands leaning on her thighs. On the other side of the bench, a homeless woman sat on the ground with her back turned; rocking back and forth. Evie stared at her, then walked through the park. A flashing diner's lights sparked Evie's attention.

"Go in there, you'll find something you like." The voice said. Evie walked toward the diner and went inside. People of all races were gathered around eating lunch. Evie hopped on the high stool at the counter.

"Well, hello." The waitress greeted Evie, placing silverware on a napkin in front of her. "Aren't you supposed to be in school?" Placing a glass of water in front of her, Evie looked at the woman's name tag.

"Early dismissal, Connie." She cracked a dry, sarcastic smile.

A young man spotted Evie and sat down next to her.

"Are you eating?" Connie asked Evie. Before she could answer, the young man interrupted. "Yes, she's eating. It's on me." Evie looked to her right and saw a brown complexioned, medium-built young man. She gazed at him, mesmerized. Connie looked at them both.

"I need to check on my other tables. I'll check back with you two in a few." Connie smiled at Evie and the young man.

"Excuse me, do I know you?" Evie questioned the stranger.

"You don't remember me?" he asked. Evie looked at him, puzzled.

"I met you a few months ago. I tried to holler at you. But you didn't give me no play."

"Your name is?"

"John." He introduced himself, extending his hand. Evie looked at it.

"John…John!" Evie said out loud, trying to remember.

"Oh! I remember you." Evie responded in a disappointed tone.

"Yeah, I saw you running out the school, so…"

Evie interrupted him, "So, you followed me?" Looking at John angrily, she twirled her seat to the left, got up and walked toward the exit.

John got up and followed her. They both left the cafe. Evie began walking quickly.

"No, I was not following you. I spotted you in the hallway and I remembered who you were. Then after I saw you run out the exit doors, I wanted to make sure you were okay." John explained, grabbing Evie's arm. She looked at him and snatched her arm back.

"Get your hands off me. First, you don't know me and second, you did follow me! Why did you chase me down, if you weren't following me? So, Mr. John, please leave me alone. I don't want to be bothered. And if you try to follow me, I'll be forced to cut you." Evie looked at him fiercely.

"Boo, there's no need for all that. Why are you so mean?" John asked.

"The world is mean?" Evie responded and walked away.

"Flash her some weed, you'll get her attention." The spirit of evil speaks to John.

"Hey, I got some of that green herb. It'll ease your tension!" John tempted Evie; she stopped walking. He caught up to her.

"It'll be our little secret," he whispered, pressing his lips to Evie's ear.

"Smoke with him. It's okay. It'll take away all your worries," the evil spirit spoke to her. Evie looked at John, cracking a smile.

"Now you're talking!" John and Evie walked out of sight, heads tilted in conversation.

Footsteps walked down the swirling marble floors. A brown hand grabbed the silver doorknob.

"Did you find her?" Mrs. Klein asked as Cory entered.

"I've looked everywhere. I even had the girls' restrooms searched out. I checked every camera and nothing."

"Where could she be?"

"She's around here somewhere. I'll go back and look at the surveillance cameras and see where she was last," Cory suggested. Mrs. Klein stood up.

"Okay, that's fine. Just let me know." She was clearly troubled. Cory looked at her, concerned, then left. Mrs. Klein walked to her door and shut it, then sat back down at her desk. Leaning back in her black leather chair, she closed her eyes with a sigh and prayed in tongues until it stopped.

"Deborah, Evie must be delivered from herself. There are many unclean spirits that drive her to do evil. If they are not cast out, they are going to destroy her," the Spirit of God interpreted.

"What are the spirits that are in Evie?" Mrs. Klein asked the Lord.

"Anger, rebellion, loneliness, lust, deceitfulness, promiscuity, suicidal thoughts; spirits that are not of Me," the Spirit of the God revealed.

"And where is she now?"

"The spirit of deceit has driven her away from her help again."

"Is Evie coming back?"

"Yes. Be still and know that I am God."

"So, do we wait here for her here?"

"No. Go home and trust the Lord your God."

Mrs. Klein raised her hands up toward heaven and waved them as tears rolled down her face. She glanced at her daughter in the picture on her desk and closed her eyes.

"I trust you, Lord! I trust you!" Mrs. Klein cried out. She opened her eyes and stared at the picture on her desk, wiping her tears.

Bishop Klein walked to his vehicle and chirped the alarm. He got into his car and pressed the ignition button. He pulled out and pressed the red on-star button.

"Call wife," Bishop said.

"Thank you for using on-star, connecting now." A loud ring came through the surround sound. The phone continued to ring and ring. "Praise the Lord, you have reached Prophetess Deborah Klein. I am unavailable to take your call." Bishop hung up, clicking off the red button.

He reached into his suit jacket, and pulled out his smart phone, pressing the screen. "Call school." The phone rang.

"Thank you for calling Kings and Queens of Faith University, this is April."

"April, this is Bishop."

"Hello, Bishop."

"By any chance is my wife in her office?" he asked.

"Actually, she is. But her door is shut. I believe I heard her in there praying."

"Okay. If she comes out, let her know that I just got out of my meeting and I will be back there shortly."

"I certainly will, Bishop. Is there anything else you need? By the way, you have several of messages."

"Thanks. I'll retrieve them when I get there," Bishop responded. "See you momentarily."

Bishop hit the off button on his touch screen phone. He drove, staring ahead.

"Something isn't right," Bishop said out loud.

"You're right. You as the Bishop must keep your house in order. I've given you Evie to shepherd her. Her blood will be on your hands if you don't bind and loose. Tonight, you must set the order in your home." The Spirit of God spoke to Bishop. He nodded his head as he continued driving.

John opened the door to his house. He entered with Evie behind him and closed the door. Evie's eyes regarded the scene.

"Where are your parents?" She asked, following John toward a door.

"My mom is at work. Come on. Let's go downstairs." John opened a door and they both walked down a long flight of stairs.

"Close the door behind you," he told Evie. John walked quickly down before Evie and turned the round beige knob on the wall. The room dimmed.

A long mixing board, keyboard with other instruments and studio equipment furnished the room. Evie admired the equipment. John opened the door to the recording room, flipping on the lights.

John invited Evie in, "Come in here." She looked around, caressing the silver microphone that hung from the ceiling.

"Do you rap?" Evie asked John. He walked around her, exiting the sound booth. Hitting a button on the switch board, a beat thumped in the room. Evie began to bop her head to the beat.

"A...one-two and one-two...can you hear me?" John spoke through the mic. Evie smiled, nodding her head.

"You ask me, do I rap..." John free-styled. . Evie began dancing in the sound booth. He stared at her. Evie started reminiscing. Her mind took her back to the strip club. Slowly Evie took off her shirt. John looked at her breasts through her lacy black bra, her honey brown skin flowing into John's view. French tipped fingernails skimmed the waist of Evie's close-fitting denim blue jeans. She worked her fingers to the front to unbutton them. John's cell phone rang. He glanced at it but kept his eyes on Evie. The familiar phone number got his attention. He stopped rapping and turned the music off. Evie continued to move.

John took the call, "What up man?" He stepped away from the microphone. Reaching for a cigar box, his dirty fingernail opened it and selected a cigar. He dug into his side pocket, pulling out a dime bag of marijuana, listening to the other side of the conversation. Slitting open the cigar with the blade, he emptied out the tobacco. John rolled the marijuana into the cigar casing. Evie danced exotically in her panties and bra. John lit the blunt. In a trance, she danced seductively, looking steadily at John, motioning him to her. He pulled hard on the blunt and a strong fire sparked at the end of it, the seeds in the cigar sizzled.

Taking in smoke, John held it for a while, then exhaled. John turned the music back on and stepped into the sound booth.

"Listen, I am in a session right now. I'll hit you up later when I am done." John hung up. Evie continued to dance with her back turned. The muscles in her back flexed with every movement. John turned her around, blowing smoke in her face. The smoke drew her nose close to his lips. He placed the blunt in her mouth, Evie grabbed it, placing her lips on the tip. She pulled hard. The blunt lit up. Inhaling, she held her breath and blew out making o's in the air. John took off his shirt, throwing it on the floor, closing and locking the booth door. John turned out the lights. Evie moaned with the music.

Isaiah, Torri, and Ruth walked past the principal's office. Bishop Klein stepped off the elevator.

"Good afternoon, Bishop Klein," Isaiah, Torri and Ruth each greeted the principal.

"Don't be late to class!" Bishop said with a smile while walking into the office.

"We won't," they called over their shoulders. The office door closed.

"Good afternoon, Bishop." April greeted him.

"Hello, April. Did she come out yet?" Bishop looked at the closed wooden door.

"No, she hasn't. I heard her crying earlier." April said. Bishop opened the door and found his wife lying on the red sofa. He stood over her.

"Deborah." At Bishop's voice, she opened her swollen eyes. She sat up and he sat next to her.

"He's back, Kenneth," Mrs. Klein sighed.

"Who's back?"

"The spirit that killed Shelia!"

"What happened while I was gone?" Bishop asked, bewildered.

"Evie left the school." Bishop looked at his wife in disbelief. He stood and walked to his desk and sat down, leaning back. Mrs. Klein walked over and sat in the wine leather chair.

"Cory took her down to be tested. She passed with a 4.0. Professor Joseph wrote a hall pass so she could return back here. He said that Evie asked him where the bathroom was. After fourth period, she was nowhere to be found. Cory viewed the cameras and saw Evie running out the G-wing exit door. He also saw John leave 10 seconds behind her." Bishop sat up in his chair.

"I've been praying since this happened. The Lord told me to be still and know that he is God. I asked him if we should look for her. He said, 'No, go home and rest.'"

Bishop sighed, "I knew something wasn't right when I was driving back here. God spoke to me and said, I must get my house in order or Evie's blood will be on my hands if I don't bind and loose some things in her life." Bishop looked at his wife.

"Yes, I believe God's word. Now I understand why the Lord wanted me to be hard on Evie earlier because of those spirits in her," Mrs. Klein said.

Bishop stared at her, concerned. "You look tired. Won't you go ahead and go home and rest? Looks like warfare has beaten my wife down today," he chuckled.

Mrs. Klein stood and walked to her desk to gather her belongings. "It's not funny," she said, her face serious. Walking toward her husband, she took her car keys out of her red purse.

"I'm not laughing at you, but at that spirit that thinks he's going to win. Jesus has already won the victory. We just have to take possession of it and take back what the devil thought he stole. So, you go ahead to the house and get some rest. Don't worry." Bishop kissed his wife, reassuring her.

"Don't worry," Mrs. Klein repeated, and cracking a smile, started to leave.

"Go straight home, Deborah. No driving around looking for Evie. God doesn't need your help." Bishop told Deborah.

She smiled, "Amen! Home is where I am going." Mrs. Klein left the office. She stopped at April's desk to converse, then exited through another set of doors. As she pressed the elevator button, Bishop watched her enter and the doors shut. He walked back into his office, picked up the receiver, dialed an extension and place the phone to his ear.

"Mrs. Santos, its Bishop. Do me a favor, can you get me John's address? Thank you. I'll be over to get it." Bishop hung up the phone. He grabbed his keys, left his office and locked it.

"April, I am leaving for the day. If any of the parents or anyone else needs to speak with me immediately, forward them to Mrs. Santos," Bishop instructed April.

"Yes, Bishop, not a problem. Enjoy the rest of your day."

"You do the same," Bishop smiled, then exited the office and walked down the hall to the main office. Sternly, he walked into Mrs. Santos office.

"Here is John Johnson's address. Is everything okay?' Mrs. Santo asked.

"Not anything I can't handle. There is one thing you can do for me, though. Call Mrs. Johnson and let her know that in order for her John to return to school, I need a conference with her immediately."

"Have all the lockers checked, including John's," the Spirit of God instructed. Bishop closed Mrs. Santos door and took a seat in front of her desk with a sigh.

"Evie and John left school together. Where they went, I am about to find out. I've already had one daughter killed by a demon, I am not about to allow any more unclean spirits take control in this school. I feel in my spirit that there is a need to check all lockers," Bishop told her.

"Check John's locker?" Mrs. Santos asked.

"Yes, I have to be obedient to the Lord," Bishop responded. They both stood and left the room.

"You go to John's house now. Have Cory, Mrs. Santos and the other security staff check every single locker in the building. Tomorrow, call a deliverance service in the chapel for every student." The Spirit of the Lord had spoken.

"Mrs. Santos, I have to leave, but you and Cory check every locker. Call in the other security officers to help you two." Mrs. Santos looked at Bishop in shock.

"I hear your thoughts. 'Bishop is crazy. There are 4,000 lockers.' Yes, I am aware. I didn't say you had to finish it today. Start tonight and you have until tomorrow. Do not inform the students. This is a random check. This must all be done after hours. Make an announcement to all coaches and extracurricular instructors. All after school activities are canceled until Thursday. Call me on my cell if you need me." Bishop walked away. Vice Principal Santos stood there with her mouth open.

"Yes, those were my words." Mrs. Santos sighed as she walked back into her office and shut the door.

CHAPTER FOUR

Leave and Don't Come Back

Evie opened the studio door. She crawled out from the dark studio room in her bra and panties, laughing.

"Yo, boo, where you going?" John stood up, flicking on the lights. His chest flexed. Evie's honey thighs moved back and forth as she crawled on her knees to the bathroom, with her clothes in her hand. The door closed. John shook his head.

"Man, you trippin!" John blasted the music.

Bishop Klein pulled up, looking suspiciously at John's house. He shut the car off. Bishop grabbed his suit jacket from the passenger side, got out, put it on, and closed the door to the luxury vehicle. He embraced the pavement, walking in authority, and rung the door bell, placing his ear to the door. Bishop stood upright and patiently waited.

"Lord, is my daughter in here?" Bishop silently questioned the Spirit of God within himself.

"Yes." The Spirit of God had spoken. Bishop rang the door bell with urgency.

"Ding dong—Ding dong—Ding Dong." Bishop released his finger from the doorbell. He paced the front porch.

Evie walked out of the bathroom fully dressed with her hair in a pony tail. She stopped by John. Typing buttons on the mixing board, John grinned. Turning his head, he looked at Evie from her feet up. The music thumped. Pulling her body close to his, he stood in front of her.

"You're not a jerk after all," Evie said.

John looked at her lips as she spoke. "I'm just a young man, looking for love," John whispered, his lips close to Evie. They kissed.

Bishop continued to ring the door bell. Finally, began to walk away, stepping down the step and away from the front door. He looked up at a window of the brick and beige panel house. He stepped back up to the front door, balling up his fists, he banged on the door.

"Lord, I thought you said she's in here!" Bishop speaks out loud. Finally, he stopped banging.

"You must trust me and lean not on your own understanding. Walk away. I will send her home." Bishop listened to the voice of God. He released his fists, dangling his hands at his side. Performing an about face while sighing with disappointment, he walked to his car.

Getting in and starting the ignition, the Bishop drove away.

John gripped Evie's butt, pulling her closer to him. He grinned and was interrupted by his cell phone. It rang and rang, eventually going it to voice mail. John put the phone in his back pocket. They kissed. Immediately, the phone rang again. John stopped kissing Evie, pulling his smart phone out of his pocket. Looking at the screen, he answered, walking away from her and turning off the music.

"Hey, mom. Oh, I'm sorry. I didn't hear my phone, I am in a session. Yeah, we had an early dismissal. You're five minutes away! I thought you had to work late? Okay, I'll be here. See you in a minute." John hung up.

"You have to leave. My mom is three minutes away," John told Evie as he grabbed her hand and pulled her toward the basement door exit.

"I thought she works late?"

"She normally does. Today, she decided to leave early and go grocery shopping." John opened the door and they proceeded up the stairs.

"Well, can I just hang around and meet your mom?" They reached the top of the stairs, John looked at her.

"Nah, I'm not gonna let you meet my mom." John laughed in Evie's face. They walked to the front door, he opened it.

Evie's body took on a questioning pose. "What do you mean by that?" Evie crossed her arms.

"Man I don't have time for this. Besides, I just don't go around introducing strange chicks to my moms." John explains looking out the front door.

"Nigga, after you got between my legs, I am some strange chick now?" Evie got up in John's face. He shoved her completely out of the house.

"You were just something to do. And I loved it! Now, I told you, my mom is on her way. Later." John slammed the door in Evie's face.

"Don't let me see you out in the streets. Nigga, you're mine." Evie screamed, kicking the front door. Evie walked away from John's house angry. She looked back.

"*Hahahahahahahaha*," Evie heard Satan laughing at her pain. She cried, walking down the street. John's mom pulled into their driveway. Evie continued to look back. Painfully, she turned her head forward, turning the corner.

The sun set as red painted toes rubbed together on the king size bed. Brown complexioned legs were crossed together, while the silk cream robe laid loosely on Mrs. Klein from her knees up; reading her Bible. The sound of her cell phone startled her. Mrs. Klein took off her black reading glasses and picked up her cell phone from the night stand on her side of the bed.

"Hello? Oh, hello, April. No, I haven't heard from Bishop since I left the school. Did you try calling his cell phone? Um...well, I'll see if I can reach him. Is everything all right?" Mrs. Klein asked.

"They what? Okay, I'll let him know. We'll deal with it in the morning. Thanks, April. Have a good evening." Mrs. Klein clicked End Call on her touchscreen, then dialed her husband's phone.

Bishop's phone rang in the empty vehicle while he stood, broken in spirit, at the cemetery, kneeling at his daughter's grave. He cried as he gazed at the tombstone:

Shelia Nichole Klein
April 8, 1988 – July 12, 2010
Beloved Daughter

"Lord you know this is very hard, especially when I'm not certain where her soul is spending eternity. But God, I trust you. Have mercy upon Evie's soul. Please do not pour your wrath out upon her, as happened with Shelia. Give her another chance, Lord. Strengthen Deborah and me to be the leaders and spiritual parents you would have us to be. Not only for Evie, Father, but for every single soul at Kings and Queens of Faith University. Lord, please hear my cry. I come to you with a broken spirit." A rain drop fell on Bishop's bald head. He stood as another rain drop fell. It began to rain.

"Go in peace, my son. All is well. For it is done. I am with you. Go home now, my son." The Spirit of God spoke. Bishop walked back to his car. Rain poured down, suddenly the cemetery became darkened. Clouds filled the city of Atlanta. Thunder and lighting roared. Bishop got in his car and drove home.

Cupping her arms over her head, Evie ran. The cold rain poured over her. Thunder clapped. She stopped running, looking ahead at the Klein's brown stone and stucco house. Evie stood there, breathing heavily.

"I really don't feel like answering to these folks," Evie spoke to herself while looking at the home from across the street.

"And you don't have to answer to them. You're nineteen. You are grown. Why don't you go and find yourself a night job at the strip club and move? You know what kind of

money you use to make." The voice of deception entertained Evie.

"You know what, I AM grown! Why am I living with them anyway? Yeah, I'm grown! I don't need anyone making decisions for me. That's what I'm going to do: pack my stuff and move out!" Evie reasoned with herself confidently, shaking her head.

"If they give you a hard time, just kill them. You'll get away with it." Satan spoke to Evie.

Evie made a devilish face, "Yeah." As she walked toward the house, lightening stuck in front of her, lighting up the entire sky. It was radiant.

Mrs. Klein walked down the stairs, thunder roared fiercely. The lights blinked. She looked at the chandelier hanging in the foyer. Gently, her feet embraced each step until she got to the bottom of the stairs. The lights went out.

"Thank you for flashlights, Lord." Mrs. Klein felt her way into the kitchen. She opened the kitchen drawer, moving her fingers around in it.

"Now I know there's a flashlight in here somewhere. Ah, there we go." Mrs. Klein picked it up, clicking the ON button as the light shone. She turned around and jumped, terrified.

"Evie. I didn't hear you come in!"

Evie just stared at her. Mrs. Klein wrapped her motherly arms around Evie, but Evie didn't move. No response. Mrs. Klein looked at Evie's wet clothes dripping on the floor and took a step back.

"I am leaving," Evie spoke boldly, displaying no emotion.

"What do you mean, you are leaving? We haven't seen you all day. We have some things we need to talk about.

And where have you been?" Mrs. Klein demanded. The electricity returned and the light flicked on. Mrs. Klein looked at Evie while Evie continued to stare at her.

"There's nothing to talk about. And, it doesn't matter where I've been. I am nineteen. I am legally grown and I don't have to go on this merry-go-round any longer." Evie walked away. Mrs. Klein followed her.

"Where are you going, Evie?" Mrs. Klein asked. Bishop Klein stepped into the open doorway. He looked at Evie as he slowly walked into the house.

"Evie! Where have you been all day?" Bishop questioned in a deep, authoritative voice. Her brown eyes stared at him rebelliously. Evie positioned her leg on the bottom step of the carpet stairs with her back to the Kleins.

"Why don't you ask your wife?!"

Bishop pushed the front door closed. He looked at Evie's back. Mrs. Klein stared at her husband while he stood next to his wife.

"I am asking you again. Where have you been?" Bishop questioned Evie a second time.

"Like I'm telling you again, ask your wife. It doesn't matter where I've been today. I don't have to answer to you or anyone. I'm grown." Evie proceeded up the stairs.

"Evie Young, turn around when I am talking to you," Bishop demanded. Evie swiftly turned around with a changed facial expression

"Go to hell!" A demonic tone rose out of Evie. The Kleins looked at one another suspiciously. Bishop Klein grabbed his wife's hand and lightly squeezed it. Evie continued up the stairs.

"You are not going anywhere. You belong to Jesus." Bishop Klein spoke boldly, then walked toward the kitchen with Mrs. Klein. Evie stopped in the middle of the stairs, evilly she turned around to an empty foyer. Evie stormed down the stairs and into the kitchen, jumping in front of the Kleins and stopping them in their tracks.

"Let me tell you something! You are not my parents and I won't allow you to tell me what to do!" Bishop and his wife looked at each other with urgency.

"In the name of Jesus, come out Satan!" Bishop spoke with authority. He stared sternly into Evie's eyes. Mrs. Klein began to pray.

"Who are you?" Bishop boldly questioned the spirit in Evie. She looked at them firmly and begin to foam at the mouth.

"I AM ANGER! ANGER WILL KILL YOU!" Evie spoke as possessed, looking at the large butcher knife in the dish rack. Mrs. Klein began to speak in tongues. She saw at what Evie was looking at. Bishop Klein quickly took off his suit jacket. Swiftly, Evie ran and grabbed the knife, running to the other side of the house out of sight.

"The Blood of Jesus, the Blood of Jesus." Bishop and Mrs. Klein began to plead. Evie began to make demonic noises. The Kleins got louder as they cautiously walked to the other side of the house.

"Ahhh!" Evie cried out. Blood hit the shiny wood floor along with the knife. Bishop Klein let go of his wife's hand, running to Evie. Blood gushed out of her arm.

"Deborah, go get a towel quickly." Bishop touched Evie on her back while she was bent over.

"Get your hands off of me," Evie spoke demonically. She stood up. Bishop looked at her. Evie's eyes began to roll around in her head. Reaching for the bloody knife, Evie bent down and her hand stretched forward. Bishop kicked it out of her reach. Evie's hand swung away, her body fell to the ground.

"In the name of Jesus, you spirit of anger and every unclean spirit, I cast you out in the name of Jesus, the Christ! Flee into the pit of hell! And I command you to never return to Evie Young." Bishop intoned. Mrs. Klein rushed in with a white towel. Stooping down quickly, she tied the towel around Evie's wrist. Bishop reached for the bottle of anointing oil on the lamp table near him. Taking off the top, Bishop poured the oil on Evie's head. He gently but firmly warned his wife to move over. Mrs. Klein began to call on the name of Jesus.

"Father, you said whatever we bind on earth is bound in heaven. And whatever we loose on earth is loosed in heaven. We bind the spirit of rebellion and we send you to the pits of hell and we command you to never return to Evie Young! And we loose from heaven, Father, your Spirit to fall upon her, quickening her mortal body, in the name of Jesus." Evie began to spit up on the wood floor, crying out.

"I speak to you, you suicide demon, come out in the Mighty name of Jesus! I command you to go to the pit of hell and don't you come back to Evie Young. I command you to loose your stronghold from her now, in Jesus's name! Lord, we thank you for your healing powers to reign upon Evie right now in the mighty name of Jesus." Bishop declared. Evie shook with some resistance. Mrs. Klein continued to call out the name of Jesus, resting her right hand on Evie's back.

"Jesus, Jesus Jesus." Evie cried out repeatedly. She placed her left hand over her mouth, puke dripping through her fingers. The white towel, drenched in blood, fell from Evie's right wrist to the wood floor. Mrs. Klein released her hand from Evie's back. Blood continued to drip from her wrist onto the towel. Bishop looked at Evie and the mess she was laying in.

"Bless your name, Lord! To God be the Glory!" Bishop continued to praise the name of the Lord. He reached into his pocket, grabbed his cell phone and dialed.

"Cory, it's Bishop. Listen, by any chance is your mom available? We have an emergency at the house. Yes, thank you. And please, have her to bring her medicine kit. We need her to stitch some things back together. Well, you'll never know what will take place during a deliverance service. Okay, thanks, Cory, we'll see her shortly." Bishop clicked off on his phone and placed it back into his pocket. Walking back toward Evie, he found his wife on her knees praying for her.

Bishop sternly looked at the two ladies and walked into another room.

CHAPTER FIVE

Prayer Works

The large silver needle sewed stitch by stitch around the bloodied wrist. Evie's arm lay straight across the silver armrest. The Kleins stood close around the doctor.

"That will just about do it," Dr. Reed proclaimed. Evie silently looked at the doctor, and then the Kleins. She turned her head in the opposite direction. Dr. Reed signaled Bishop and Mrs. Klein into the hallway. They left Evie's room, closing the door shut.

"Thank you so much for coming out this late. Thank God for school physicians!" Mrs. Klein smiled and shook Dr. Reed's hand in appreciation. Bishop shook her hand with a smile.

"Not a problem. You both are welcome. She really did a number on her wrist. Thank God she didn't hit an artery.

Another half inch and she would have bled to death. Has she always been suicidal?"

"Truthfully, Evie has been through a hard, rough life. But I thank God for sending her our way. She's going to make it." Mrs. Klein spoke with a catch in her voice. "The spirit of suicide can form itself against her, but it shall not prosper in her life. As a matter of fact, from this day forward, in the name of Jesus, we cancel every plot Satan seeks to form," Mrs. Klein said to Dr. Reed as she smiled weakly.

"Yes, I agree. Amen." Dr. Reed closed her eyes, nodding her head in agreement. "Well, let me get going. I have a long day ahead of me." Dr. Reed proceeded down the carpeted stairs and stopped in the middle of the hall.

The Kleins followed. "Dr. Reed, thank you again. Will you be in tomorrow, or are you on call?" Bishop asked.

"I have a couple of rounds to make at the hospital. But I will be back at the school about noon." Dr. Reed paused in thought, staring at the Kleins. "Bishop, Mrs. Klein, I've been wondering if you'd allow me to counsel Evie. With the life you've both described she's had, there's so much that is bottled up within her. Binding influential spirits is great, but we have to get to the root of this problem so that her behavior can reflect healing." The Kleins look at each other and nodded in agreement.

"That sounds like a plan, Doc. You just let us know when," Bishop Klein responded with a smile. Dr. Reed shook their hands.

"When I get to the school tomorrow, I'll check my schedule and see when I can meet with her." Dr. Reed said reassuringly while she walked toward the exit.

"Kenneth, can you walk Dr. Reed to the door? I'm going back in here with Evie." Mrs. Klein pointed to Evie's room. Bishop nodded in agreement.

Gazing at the right side of the wall, Evie stared in thought. Mrs. Klein gently closed the door. Walking over to her bed, Evie's eyes scrolled back and forth without her head moving. Mrs. Klein sat next to her. Evie resumed staring at the wall.

"How are you feeling?" Mrs. Klein asked her. Evie didn't respond. Mrs. Klein sighed. "We received your test results. You scored more than 95% on every section. You are a very bright young lady, Evie. Out of all the years Kenneth and I have been principals, it is very rare to see a student score, an 'A' on every subject area. That truly blessed my soul." Mrs. Klein smiled gently, looking for a response.

"Evie, the point I am trying to make is this: you are a very gifted young lady with a very high IQ. Our desire is to see God's very best manifest within you. I know you've been hearing this from us over and over again. We just want you to know that we love you." She gently touched Evie's arm.

"Please say something," Mrs. Klein insisted. Evie's eyes roamed away from the wall. Slowly, she turned her head.

"What is there to say? Pain has numbed me." Evie's eyes filled with tears as she stared at Mrs. Klein.

"Evie, I understand."

"Do you really? It's typical for a person to say, 'I understand what you are going through.' But until you've been me, and breathed me, you have no clue. You may have an idea, the same way we have an idea of what Jesus went through on the cross. But we can only imagine. So, no, you don't understand. Just say you have an idea because you really don't know," Evie shook her head and then looked away.

"Evie, you are absolutely correct. Only God knows the heart of mankind. But what I know is I am looking at a caterpillar who is destined to become a butterfly. There is greatness in you, Evie, in spite of all the tribulations and pain you've encountered." She smiled gently at Evie.

Evie turned her head, looked toward Mrs. Klein, and then sat up in bed. "My dreams and vision in life have faded. Graduating high school and going to college to study law was my goal."

"And you can still do those things, Evie! It's not too late! God says in his word, in Psalms 37:4, '**Delight yourself also in the LORD; and he shall give you the desires of your heart**.' The desires of your heart, baby, will be fulfilled after you have aligned yourself according to God's plans for your life. His desires for your life will then become yours. He wants you to dream. He is the One who placed those dreams in you! Let Him become the dream fulfiller. How do you do that? Through relationship and communing with the Father." Mrs. Klein scooted closer to Evie, grabbing a Bible from the night stand. Evie watched Mrs. Klein's fingertips flick through the pages.

"Let's see here. John Chapter 10, starting at verse 8: '**All that ever came before me are thieves and robbers: but the sheep did not hear them. I am the door: by me if any man enter in, he shall be saved, and shall go in and out, and find pasture.**' Mrs. Klein looked up from reading.

"What the scripture is teaching us is that before accepting Christ into our lives, we were subject to Satan. But when you are in Christ Jesus, you become His sheep and He becomes your Great Shepherd. And because Christ is the door that you shall live in, breathe in, walk in and move in, you will find rest. The thief is Satan, whom you will no longer listen to or entertain his lies. The Spirit of the Lord is saying that it is only through Christ that you will be safe! He is the door to your abundant life. He is the only way, and only through Him shall man enter in and be saved. Satan is a thief. He comes and tries to steal your peace, joy, hope, and dreams. But it is Jesus who comes to enter into your heart and gives you life and life more abundantly, beyond what you can ever imagine."

"But I feel so far away from God. I just feel like He doesn't hear me." Evie explained while Mrs. Klein turned the pages in the Bible.

"Here read this, Psalms 139:8." She gave Evie the Bible.

"If I ascend up into heaven, thou *art* there: if I make my bed in hell, behold, thou art there." Evie looked up from reading and stared at Mrs. Klein.

"God is omnipresent," Mrs. Klein said, smiling. "He is present everywhere, and this is so we are never lost. Those who are saved and live by his Spirit remain in the presence of God. But for those who run with Satan and have made their beds there, God is still not too far away to hear their cries. He loves you more than you love yourself, beyond what you can ever imagine, Evie! When you hurt, He hurts. When you cry, God is right there, bottling up every tear. Have you noticed that out of all the times Satan has tried to devour you, that none of those times has he prospered? Why, the hand of God intervenes and says,

'Not so! She belongs to Me.' Have you noticed that?" Evie nodded her head in agreement.

"That's all because God loves you. He has never left you, nor forsaken you. We are the ones who leave and walk away from Him. That is why the scripture said, "**If you make your bed in hell, behold I am there**," because He never went anywhere, we did! God remains in the same place, waiting for us to return to His path of righteous living. When we are in our mess, God sees it but He's not too far away. He is a holy God who remains in a holy place. When we sin, we wander away from that place, out of His presence. But when you call on the Savior's name, a gracious name, with a repenting heart and a changed mind, God will answer. I believe when I first met you and ministered to you in the motel, the Lord had me to mention to you then that He is with you." Mrs. Klein's eyes smiled at Evie.

"Yes, I remember," Evie replied.

"So, let not your heart be troubled. But rest in Him." Deborah Klein continued a soft, motherly tone.

"Why hasn't God responded to my prayers when I ask him about my parents?" Evie asked. Mrs. Klein stared at her thoughtfully and then turned to the scriptures.

"John 9:31 reads, **'Now we know that God hears not sinners: but if any man be a worshiper of God, and does his will, him he hears.'** When a person is in habitual and repetitious sin and is against the truth of God's word, and they desire to remain in sin, God will keep that sinner right where they desire to be. He doesn't override a person's choice. See, Evie, God heard you when your heart yearned for direction. He stepped in and saved you. But when it comes down to specific prayers that require a closer walk and worship to receive a greater revelation of what you've prayed for, God has his appointed time for those answered prayers. Does that make sense to you?"

"Yes, it does," Evie answered.

"Here's a better way to describe it: if God is continually sending his messengers to help and warn a person to turn from their wicked ways, yet that person chooses to do the same thing over and over again with a hardened heart, God won't grant that person's prayers. He can't because that person is so far away from Him and out of jurisdiction of His benefits. In Romans 3:23, the Bible says, **"For all have sinned, and fall short of the glory of God**," but we shall return to right standing with Him because we have invited the Holy Spirit who helps us to dwell within us. A sinner is unable to do those things. For one, they do not have the Holy Spirit, which leaves them unheard for specific requests. You have invited Christ back into your life and asked that God's mercy and grace embrace you. He has heard your request. Now you must be patient and allow him to solve the mystery," Mrs. Klein encouraged her. Evie glanced down at the Bible while Mrs. Klein turned the pages.

"Here's another great passage: Matthew 7:7- 11 says, **'Ask, and it shall be given you; seek, and you shall find; knock, and it shall be opened unto you: for every one that asks, receives, and he that seeks; and to him that knocks it shall be opened. Or what man is there of you, whom if his son ask bread, will he give him a stone? Or if he asks for a fish, will give him a serpent? If you then, being evil, know how to give good gifts to your children, how much more shall your Father which is in heaven give good things to them that ask him?"** Mrs. Klein closed the Bible and placed it back on the night stand. She took both of Evie's hands.

"Evie, you are now a daughter of the Kingdom of Heaven. God will not withhold any good thing from you, baby. He first loved you. Anything you ask for and desire in Christ Jesus will be fulfilled. The mystery of your parents God will unfold in time, but first He would like to reveal Himself to you personally, so that you will truly know Him without a shadow of a doubt. You've already prayed. Now receive in your heart by faith that your prayers are already answered. Now you are just waiting for the manifestation to be released in the natural world. Amen?"

"Amen," Evie responded with a slight grin. Mrs. Klein smiled broadly.

"Ask Evie where she was today," The Spirit of God instructed Mrs. Klein.

"Evie...," Mrs. Klein looked at Evie with concern. "Where did you go after you took your test today?"

Evie looked at her fearfully. "I left the school." She hesitated to continue, then sighed and blinked her eyes. "I...I went to a diner. John followed me from the school and then..." Evie sighed, struggling to continue.

The Spirit of God flashed visions of Evie and John to Mrs. Klein. She cringed, "Say no more, Evie. You just received the word of God. Now I encourage you to apply it to your life. Please don't take what I just shared lightly. Apply it, and no more playing games with your salvation. Now it is time to walk it out, and Bishop and I are here to guide you through. Amen?" Mrs. Klein looked at Evie seriously.

"Amen," Evie agreed.

"Well, we'll see you in the morning, bright and early." Mrs. Klein smiled and kissed her on the forehead.

"Yes, ma'am. Good night," Evie replied with a relieved grin. Deborah walked to the door, looking over her shoulder at Evie.

"Good night," said Mrs. Klein and she left the room.

Evie took a deep breath. Gazing toward the ceiling, tears began to roll down her cheeks. She shook her head in distress. Evie pulled back the brown comforter. She swung her legs from under the brown and white striped sheets. She fell to her knees and lowered her face to the floor.

"God, please forgive me from all of my sins and shortcomings. I need You like never before. For me, this is hard, but for You, it's easy. Come into my life and save me again. Hear my cry, Lord." She lifted her head and grabbed the comforter from the bed. Her face was drenched in tears. She held both edges of the comforter and tucked herself underneath, prostrate on the floor.

CHAPTER SIX
Divine Intervention

Torri rested peacefully. Her white silk sheet covered her. A cool breeze of midnight air drifted through her room. The sheer beige curtains billowed gently.

"Wake up, beloved." The still voice of God spoke. Torri opened her eyes, blinking. She looked at the digital clock next to her bed. 12:00 a.m.

"Those that seek me early shall find me. I want to talk to you, Torri."

"Now Lord?" Torri asked.

"Yes. Now."

"Okay, Lord. I am all yours. I am listening." Torri closed her eyes, drifting back into sleep. She breathed deeply.

"Torri!"

Torri swiftly sat up.

"Yes Lord, I am up." Torri rubbed her eyes and stretched, pulling her covers back. Swinging her legs off the bed, she lowered herself to her knees.

"God, I bless you. Lord, I thank you for waking me up. You are worthy to receive all of the praises, Father. I love you, Lord. For I love to seek your face. I am all yours. My heart, my mind; my soul belong to you. Whatever you want me to say, Lord, I'll say. Whatever you want me to do, I'll do. And wherever you want me to go, I will go. Send me, Lord." Torri prays to the Spirit of the God, then she falls silent.

"You must go and visit your cousin. You must go and give her my last warning. Once you have done that, her blood will no longer be on your hands."

"But Lord, You know she's not going to listen to me!"

"You speak what I tell you to speak. And if it's not received, you shake the dust off your feet. If you choose not to, her blood will be on your hands."

Torri sighed.

"Torri, did lies roll off your tongue when you said, Send me, Lord? Do you belong to Me? Does your heart really mean what your tongue speaks?" the Spirit of the Lord asked. Torri lifted her head toward the ceiling, closing her eyes. She took a deep breath.

"When am I supposed to go?" Torri asked.

"Tomorrow, after school. I want you to fast. Only drink water, until sunset. . I will fill you up with My words."

"Yes, Lord. Thank you, Jesus. And even right now, I ask You to have mercy upon my cousin, oh God. You are a God of second chances, and I thank you."

"Yes, I am a Father who is full of grace and mercy. And yes, I am a God of second chances. But there comes a time and a season where grace and mercy run out for sinners without a heart of repentance and I turn them over to experience the consequences of their reprobate minds. So you go and obey me, daughter, that your hands shall be washed clean."

Torri nodded her head in agreement, lifting her hands up.

"Torri, I see your heart. I know your battles of the flesh. Continue to live by My Spirit. I know you desire Isaiah and he desires you. But it's not time. Remain faithful and holy unto Me; pray in secret and I shall reward you openly. He knows that you are the one chosen for him. But you must let me bring you together, not you, yourselves. Just wait on me. I will do it, in the right season, if you faint not." The Spirit of the Lord continued to speak to Torri. She wept.

"Yes, Lord. I love Isaiah with my whole heart. He is such a beautiful friend who reminds me of You. Of course, no one could ever take Your place. But I trust You regarding him and I have a love that is unspeakable for him."

"I know, daughter. I placed that love for Isaiah in you. What I put together, let no man tear apart. Just wait on me and I will meet every desire of your heart. Isaiah loves you with the same measure. But it's not time yet. You stay focused on Me, and I, the Lord your God, will bless you both."

"Amen," Torri responded, smiling.

A vision of Evie weeping flashed before her eyes. Torri fell face down to the floor. She prayed in tongues and wept, groaning.

"You are sensing what Evie is experiencing. Begin to pray for her strength. I am going to restore your friendship with her," spoke the Spirit of the Lord. Torri sat up on her knees, wiping the tears from her eyes.

"Lord, help me to understand what happened to Evie's family," Torri asked God.

"It's a mystery, Torri, only I can and will solve. Divine intervention will reveal all things hidden. Begin to intercede on behalf of Evie's strength and her family. The mystery will unfold in time."

"Thank you, Lord . You said whatever is hidden shall be brought to light. Thank you in advance, Father , for putting all the pieces together. Restore Evie, Lord. Teach her Your voice, oh God, and the voice of a stranger she shall and will not follow.

"Get on Facebook, you will find Evie's brother." The Spirit of the Lord directed. Torri's face lit up. She got up, walked over to her computer and sat down. Gently, grabbing the glass shelf, Torri slid out her white keyboard. Tapping a key, Torri started the computer. She typed in her password, pressed enter, and Evie and Torri's youth picture displayed as her screen saver. Torri logged into Facebook.

"Look up Justin Sanders-Young," the Spirit of God instructed.

She typed into the search bar, 'Justin Sanders-Young,' and pressed enter. Different people with the name Justin Sanders popped up.

"Here we go, Justin Sanders-Young." Torri clicked on Justin's profile. She then click on info. Slowly she read his information.

"This is him!" Torri clicked on friend request then reluctantly clicked the message icon.

"Not yet, Torri. Send him a message after he accepts your request." Torri agreed, attempting to click off of Facebook, but she received an instant message.

"What are you doing up so late?" Isaiah typed.

"Lol, I was about to ask you the same thing! ☺ I just got out of prayer." Torri typed back.

"Lolol, prayer on FB?" Isaiah responded.

"You have jokes, I see, lol. FYI, Jesus and I just got out of an intimate conversation, Mr. Nosy..lol," Torri replied.

"I'm jealous…☹" Isaiah typed.

"You should be! Nah, the Lord woke me up about an hour ago to go into prayer. Afterward, he laid on my spirit to look up Evie's brother, Justin." Torri shared, looking below the message box, she saw that Isaiah was typing.

"Did you find him?"

"Yes. I sent him a friend request. Now I am just waiting for him to confirm."

Torri continued, "I know that God is going to unfold this mystery and reveal the truth behind all of this. We have to continue to keep Evie lifted up in prayer."

"Of course. Not only that, she really needs you spiritually and naturally. You two have known each other since childhood. So it's no coincidence you both have crossed paths again, in Georgia at that. God has divinely orchestrated your footsteps. And with you being the stronger one spiritually, you must continue to intervene and be there for her. She needs you," Isaiah stressed.

"You're right and I am. Like I said, when I was in prayer, the Holy Spirit instructed me to find Justin, so agree and pray that he responds."

"Lol…it's funny. Right before I was led to get online, God had me in prayer as well. He had me interceding for Evie and her relationship with Him. God wants to speak to Evie himself and teach her His voice. One thing I do know in this season is God is truly calling His sons and daughters into a more intimate and closer relationship with Him. What God showed me is Satan's heat has been turned up. Those who are distracted by the cares of the world or seek first other gods for a solution instead of the Most High and

Only God will be deceived. And I believe God wants us to help disciple Evie by keeping her close like Jesus kept his disciples close to Him. Besides, God doesn't want Evie to be deceived anymore."

"Wow. You preach, Prophet Isaiah! Is that the reason why I love you, because of your wisdom, knowledge and your thirst for God?" Torri smiled and pressed enter.

"Is it? You must decipher that lol," Isaiah responded.

"It has already been, Mr. Isaiah… Yes, I love you because of all those things and more. I was praying about you just a few moments ago. It was a nice prayer, xoxox….lol." Torri blushed as she pressed enter.

"Really…umm…divine intervention, because I was praying for you 2 ." Isaiah smirked and pressed enter.

"Are you flirting with me?" Torri asked.

"Yes, I am. And if we were married already, we wouldn't be on the internet going back and forth. I'd be doing a lot more than flirting."

"Married!?!" Torri typed with a shocked expression.

"Torri, we both know that God has placed us together. There's such a divine connection between you and me. The past year of knowing you, you helped me to understand God at another level," Isaiah explained.

"Really! How?" Torri asked.

"You are a woman with such great virtue, high morals, and a drive to go higher with God. So I have to stay on my toes and come up higher in order to even think of trying to pursue a woman such as you…☺."

"Wow. Isaiah, that is so sweet!" Torri blushed.

"Torri, I know the other day when I kissed you some things got hot. And one thing I never want us to do is to allow temptation to take us out of the perfect will of God."

"I agree, and that is one of the things I was praying about. I'm going to be real with you. When you kissed me the other day, I got so excited I felt like I sinned against God. So yeah, we're going to have to find another way to express what we both are feeling inside. Maybe I can draw you a big heart, you can cut it out and glue it to your forehead...lolol." Torri giggled and pressed enter.

"Lol...No! We'll find another way. Can we do a late lunch tomorrow after school?"

"Tomorrow is not good.☹ The Lord has me on an assignment that I must take care of. And no, I can't tell you what it is until I've accomplished my mission ... lol."

"Gee...thanks for answering my question before I ask...lol." Isaiah smiled and pressed enter.

"I know you! Remember, we are divinely connected." Torri grinned and clicked enter. "But Friday I am all yours☺." Torri typed and pressed send.

"Friday, it is! Well, we have classes in a few hours. Time to turn in. See you in the morning, beautiful!" Isaiah replied with a heart emoji.

"Good night, my man of God." Torri sent a heart emoji.

"I love you, Torri." Isaiah typed and got offline before she could reply. With a smile, she walked away from her computer, got into bed, and pulled the covers over her. "Father, you set me up!" She smiled, closing her eyes.

CHAPTER SEVEN

Obedience Wins

Rays of sun beamed through the white blinds. A mild breeze traveled in from the slightly opened window, as the sheer white curtains stirred.

"Evie, honey, we have to get to the school early this morning!" Mrs. Klein called from downstairs. The bathroom door opened. Evie walked out into the bedroom. Grabbing her purse with her left hand, she placed it on her shoulder while looking in the mirror.

"I'm ready!" Evie fixed the sling strap on her left shoulder as her right arm rested in it. Her left hand opened the bedroom door. Honey brown, sexy legs strutted the catwalk to the stairwell. Evie's 3-inch black sandals embraced the carpet steps down to the landing. Her black knee-length skirt flowed around her. Evie turned right into the kitchen and through the garage. She walked through the open door to the running car; Bishop Klein got out from the driver's side. He opened the back door for Evie. Evie took her seat. He closed the door behind her. Getting back in, he placed the vehicle in reverse, the garage door opened and the vehicle rolled smoothly down the driveway. The garage door closed. Shifting the car into drive, he drove off.

"Well, you look mighty beautiful this morning. You are glowing!" Mrs. Klein turned around, looking at Evie in the back seat. "You look as if you've had one night with the king!" Bishop Klein glanced through the rearview mirror with a smile. She smiled back at them both.

"Yeah." Evie smiled, and looked down at her bandaged arm.

"How does your wrist feel?" Deborah Klein asked.

"A little sore."

"Once we get to school and get you your schedule, Bishop will run and pick up the prescription from Dr. Reed. She said you'll have some pain through the healing process. But the pain pill will help numb the nerves," she smiled.

"Okay," Evie replied softly, leaning her head back and closing her eyes. Mrs. Klein grinned and turned back around, enjoying the ride.

"Beep, beep." Ruth honked the car horn.

"Where is this girl?" Ruth honked the horn again.

Torri burst through the front door of her dorm house. She ran in her red heels to the car, grabbed the silver handle and got in.

"And why are you blowing the horn like you are in the hood?" Torri joked with a smile. Ruth drove off.

"You are the one who's moving like Pookies' grandmother with corns on her feet; like we have all day. That's why," Ruth joked back. "I have a taste for some cappuccino before class, and you are slowing me down."

"Okay, then! Are you sure your daddy is not black?" Torri jokingly inquires.

"Maybe!" Ruth laughs.

"Okay, so listen. Early this morning when I was in prayer, the voice of God instructed me to look up Evie's brother, Justin." Torri shared.

"So, what happened?"

"I sent him a friend request on Facebook. I'm just waiting for him to confirm."

"Do you think he'll know where Evie's parents are?" Ruth asked.

"I'm not sure. Surely he's a link somehow if the Spirit of the Lord instructed me to look him up. Be in prayer with me about that," Torri requested.

"Yes, ma'am!" Ruth pulled up to the gas station.

"Oh, and I'm going to need a favor from you today," Torri asked.

"Ah-oh, no drive-bys! We almost got caught last time!" Ruth laughed, placing the car in park.

"Did you take a silly pill this morning?" Torri asked, surprised.

"Yes, I did, and don't spoil it! Okay, for real what's the favor?" Ruth asked.

"My other instruction was that I have to go see my cousin today after school," Torri replied.

"Oh!" Ruth looked at Torri.

"And I need you to go with me."

Ruth made a face.

"Please…?" Torri begged.

"I need about three cappuccinos now! One for the Father, one for the Son, and one for the Holy Spirit, to help me say yes." Ruth replied, rolling her eyes with a smirk. Both ladies got out of the vehicle.

"Aw, come on. It will be an experience!" Torri said, both ladies approached the store entrance.

"Wrong! It will be an experience for you! I'm just coming as support. I'm staying in the car. Besides, you're the one who has to do the dirty work, not me." Ruth asserted. Torri placed her arm around her waist as they entered the store.

Second floor, third floor, fourth floor, the elevator slowed down and the doors opened. Bishop, Mrs. Klein and Evie exited. Bishop Klein unlocked the main office door. Everyone entered, and then he unlocked the inner office. Evie walked in and took a seat in the main office.

"Evie, come in here, dear, so we can go over your schedule." Mrs. Klein suggested, sitting at her desk. Unenthused, Evie complied. She sat down in front of Mrs. Klein's desk.

"Before I print out your schedule for the rest of the year, I would like to go over it with you, okay?" Mrs. Klein smiled at Evie. Bishop typed on his computer.

"Sure," Evie said softly.

"As I mentioned to you yesterday, you scored well on your evaluation test. High enough that we are placing you in advanced classes. You will be a senior with college courses. I'm going to print out your schedule and let you take a look at it. If you have any questions, let me know." Mrs. Klein hit print on her computer. Standing up from her desk, she walked to the printer to retrieve the printout. Bishop Klein stood up from his desk. He smiled at Evie.

"Evie, here you go." Mrs. Klein handed the schedule to her.

"Thank you," Evie responded. Hesitantly, she looked up at Bishop and Mrs. Klein.

"Um … I just wanted to say thank you both for everything. I truly thank God for you guys. After praying last night, God helped me to realize that He has given me purpose. You both were placed in my life to help me get to my final destination. This morning when I was getting dressed, I peeked under my bandages to see how Satan was trying to take me out, and I've made up in my mind that enough is enough. I am ready to fight back. So whatever I have to do to learn that Bible and walk a righteous walk before God, I am ready. I will no longer be the devil's advocate. He split my family apart, and then he has tried to destroy me mentally and physically. But no more!" Evie proclaimed. Mrs. Klein stood speechless with tears in her eyes.

"Glory to your name, Lord." Bishop praised God.

"Evie, you keep your eyes focused on the Lord. Keep walking with him. There is so much God has in store for you. The key is staying connected to the rest of God's body, people who will pour wisdom and strength into you, encourage you, lead and guide you. That is what we are here for. My wife and I are not your enemies. We love you as our very own and we know that God is going to unfold the truth concerning your biological parents. And we also know that it's going to take some time for you to adjust. You've gotten into the habit of not trusting anyone. But I encourage you, daughter, put your trust in the Lord. Stay on your knees. God will line everything up for you." Bishop smiled at Evie with compassion. He hugged her. Mrs. Klein smiled. Tears built up in Evie's eyes.

"I am sorry for giving you two such a hard time. Bishop, you couldn't have said it any better. I don't trust anyone. I have one voice telling me one thing, another voice telling me another until I don't know what or who to believe," Evie explained.

"Evie, as you continue to spend time with the Lord, you will know his voice and a voice of a stranger you shall and will not follow. It's a process. And as Bishop said, staying connected to people who are part of the body of Christ is the key. Iron sharpens iron," Mrs. Klein shared with Evie.

"Good morning." April peeked her head into their office. Bishop greeted her with a smile.

"Good morning, April," Mrs. Klein greeted her.

"Bishop, we've completed what you asked us to do yesterday evening. There are five large bags locked up in the VP's office." April explained. Bishop looked troubled.

"Deborah, let all the calls forward to our office. April and I are going to Mrs. Santos office. I'll radio you when I get there. After the bell rings for first period, I need you to meet me there."

"Okay." Mrs. Klein replied with concern. April and Bishop exit the office.

Torri and Ruth walked down the hallway with the other students. Torri stopped at her locker. Ruth stops further down at hers.

"You're my sunshine on a cloudy day." Isaiah stood on the side of Torri's locker singing, while she stooped down to get her book.

"Good morning. How are you?" Torri stood up from her knees with a smile, grabbing her books. She closed her locker. Isaiah smiled, kissing Torri on the cheek.

"I am excellent and have some excellent research I've discovered," Isaiah smiled as they walked down the hallway.

"Really?" Torri inquired with a smile.

"Well, after I finished chatting with you online, the Lord led me to backtrack ten years of the people who have been missing." Isaiah and Torri stops in front of the class room. Isaiah goes into his note book pulling out a stack of printed documents. He hands them to Torri.

"Missing people?" Torri looks puzzled.

"Evie's parents!" Isaiah explains. Torri's face lights up in rememberance. The bell rings. Students walks around Torri and Isaiah; entering into the class room.

"Oh Isaiah thank you." Torri replies.

"Don't thank me. The Lord has placed it heavy on my spirit that we have to be there for Evie for real. God is up to something and the truth about her parents is about to be revealed." Isaiah and Torri enter the classroom and take their seats across from each other. Isaiah looked at John's empty desk. Other students continued to enter and sit down. Minister Klein II wrote on the board.

"We'll go over it later," Isaiah whispered to Torri.

"Okay," Torri replied with a smile.

"Good morning, everyone. We're going to continue where we left off yesterday, talking about human consciousness." As Minister Klein walked toward his desk, his mother walked in with Evie. Torri and Evie locked eyes. Isaiah glanced at Torri while copying the lesson from the board.

"Good Morning, Prophetess Klein." Minister Klein greeted his mother and Evie with a smile. Evie smirked.

"Good morning, Minister Klein," Mrs. Klein addressed her son. "Can I speak with you in the hallway?"

"Class, start copying the lesson for today, while I step out for a moment." Minister Klein, his mother and Evie stepped into the hallway. Mrs. Klein closed the door behind them.

"Evie will be in your class for Bibical Psychology this semester. Evie, this is Minister Kenneth Klein the II, my son. He is one of the finest professors on campus – not because he's my son, but because God anointed and qualified him. So you are in good hands. Now I have to get to Mrs. Santos's office. Radio me if you need anything. Okay, Ms. Evie, I would like to officially welcome you to Kings and Queens of Faith University!" Mrs. Klein smiled and hugged Evie.

"See you later!" Mrs. Klein walked down the hallway with her walkie-talkie in her hand. Evie and Minister Klein went back into the classroom. Standing with Evie in front, Evie stared at Torri briefly, then looked around at the class at everyone there.

"Everyone, this is Evie Young. She will be joining us for the remaining of this semester. Evie, you can take a seat wherever one is available." Minister Klein replied. Evie walked down the middle of the room. Torri and Evie continued to make eye contact. Evie sadly walked past her, sitting in the very back row.

"Lord, help me!" Evie said to herself with a sigh.

"Okay, you all should have written down the lesson for today. For those who haven't, you will have an opportunity to do so 15 minutes before the bell rings. Yesterday, we were discussing the human makeup. Today, we are going to get into depth about understanding human consciousness. That is what the world calls it. God created everything under the sun, by speaking it into existance. All throughout the Bible, you will find that God speaks to his people. Then, you will also see how Satan speaks. It began in the Garden of Eden, and it continues up to today. And then, you have your own voice, which is your own will. With these three voices, people battle every day trying to understand who is leading them. If you are dealing with the spirit of confusion, Satan is in the midst.

God is not the author of confusion." Evie's face lit up, attentive to Minister Klein's lesson. He continued.

Bishop and Mrs. Santos were sitting in her office. Mrs. Klein entered.

"I made it as quick as possible." Mrs. Klein said slowly looking at the large black trash bags in the office. "What's going on?" she asked, bewildered.

"The Spirit of the Lord instructed me to do a random check through every locker in this building. And I am very disturbed at what we've found," Bishop Klein told her. "Look!"

He showed Mrs. Klein what was in the bag. Shock covered her face as she pulled out labeled baggies of condoms, marijuana, prescription drugs, and cigarettes. Mrs. Klein looked up at Mrs. Santos and then her husband.

"You found all of this in our high school students' lockers?!"

"That is just bag number one," Mrs. Santos said while she reached into her desk drawer, pulled out a handkerchief and laid it on the desk. Mrs. Klein looked at her as Mrs. Santos looked at what was in the handkerchief. Stunned, she placed her right hand over her chest.

"Whose locker did you find this in?" Mrs. Klein asked.

"Mrs. Santos, Ms. Johnson is here," Mrs. Santos' secretary informed her.

"Send her in." Mrs. Santos responded. Mrs. Klein looked at Bishop as she slowly walked over and sat next to him. John and his mother entered the office. Mrs. Santos stood up from her desk to greet Ms. Johnson, shaking her hand. Bishop and Mrs. Klein stood to shake her hand as well, while Mrs. Santos walked over and shut her office door. Mrs. Santos looked at John as she took a seat at her desk.

John looked at the gun wrapped in a handkerchief on the desk.

"Ms. Johnson, we called you in today on two matters that are very serious. Yesterday, John skipped class and left the school. We have it on camera." Mrs. Santos said.

"I would like to ask John, when you left the school yesterday, where did you go?" Bishop asked in a serious tone.

"His answer is a lie. Don't be deceived," The Spirit of the Lord said to Bishop Klein.

"I had an emergency," John said. The principals looked at one another.

"What emergency did you have that was so important for you to skip school?" John's mother looked at him questioningly.

"Well, you know I've been waiting on this record deal, so my boy called me and said that he was going out of town.

And the only time I could meet him was during noon, so I left," John responded. Mrs. Klein scratched her head.

"John, look at me! You are lying. Tell the truth! You left the school to chase after my spiritual daughter and then you took her back to your mother's house and took advantage of her!" Bishop revealed.

"John, you got to be kidding me! And I know this could bc true because Chantell and Lisa were the last two you got caught with in my house! I told you, boy, I am so sick of your behavior! You just don't listen." John looked at his mother and gritted his teeth in shame.

"Now let's hear your story again, John; the truth?" Mrs. Klein asked. John looked at her angrily.

"John?" Ms. Johnson looked at her son for an explanation.

"Man, the hell with school! I don't need any fake principals, bishops or teachers questioning me." John crossed his arms and slouched in his chair. Mrs. Klein shook her head. Bishop stood to his feet with a disturbed demeanor, walking toward Mrs. Santos desk. Mrs. Klein looked at her husband with her brows furrowed.

"John, we found this in your locker. Can you tell us about this?" Mrs. Santos asked in a firm tone. John's mother turned around, looking at John face-to-face. Bishop picked up the phone, dialed and walked away, speaking softly. John looked at Bishop.

"John? A gun! Where did you get this from, or should I say who?" His mother questioned him.

"It's one of my friends'," John responded nonchalantly. Bishop put down the phone and sat on the edge of Mrs. Santos' desk. He looked at John sternly.

"John, you know school policy. It's in the student hand book. No weapons, drugs, cigarettes or any dangerous conduct on school premises. So for that gun to get past security is a serious violation. And this is not the first incident with you! Three months ago, we found marijuana on you and we gave you warning. One month prior to that, you had a similar situation like the one with my daughter. And then today, John, we're trying to get answers out of you and you are not telling us the truth. So I am asking you this, Mr. Johnson, what do you think we should do about this situation?"

"Man, I don't know. Whatever. At this point, who cares about school? John said rebelliously.

His mother slapped him. Mrs. Santos and Mrs. Klein reacted with shocked surprise. "Boy, you better have some respect! I am tired of coming up to this school," said Mrs. Johnson, sitting on the edge of her seat.

Bishop looked up at the front door, then stood up. "John, since you don't know what we should do about the situation, I guess that just leaves me to make the decision according to the word of God. We must obey the laws of the land and we must follow the student handbook. You brought a weapon on school premises." Bishop stated.

Cory walked in with two officers. Everyone stood up. John looked at the officers angrily. The officers approached him.

"John, mercy has run out for you. And since you've failed to have any intention of cooperating with us, you leave us with no other choice but to report this to the authorities. I can't allow this behavior to go on in this school, from you or any other student. We warned you months ago about your behavior. Take him. I'm sorry, Mrs. Johnson," Bishop spoke sadly. He walked out of the office.

The officers arrested John. His mother stood there, speechless and in tears, with her hand over her mouth, sobbing. John glared hatefully at everyone in the office. The officers left with him. Mrs. Santos and Mrs. Klein looked at each other. Mrs. Klein took Ms. Johnson by the arm and walked her out the door.

"Mrs. Santos, Bishop said to make a special announcement for all students and teachers to report to the dome after fourth period," her secretary informed her.

"Okay, thank you. Please close my door." Mrs. Santos requested. Her secretary silently nodded and closed the door.

CHAPTER EIGHT
The Truth Unfolds

Bishop walked down five flights of brick stairs, away from the school. He looked both ways and crossed the street. Troubled, he sat on the green bench.

"God, what have I done?" Bishop asked, full of guilt. "Lord, was I wrong for what I've done?"

"Condemnation isn't of the Lord you know." His wife walked up and sat beside him on the bench. He looked at her sadly.

"You are out here because …," Mrs. Klein looked for an explanation.

"Although school policy is our guide, when do we bend it for the sake of protecting our students?" Bishop asked.

"Kenneth, we have bent our policy every which way for our students, especially John. Having an unlicensed gun on the premises is illegal and dangerous! And had you not done that, and let it slide, our position as leaders would've been out of order. It was the Holy Spirit that moved you to call the police. It's called "wisdom," dear." Mrs. Klein looked lovingly at his face.

"So why do I feel so guilty?" Bishop asked his wife.

"Ask God to search your heart regarding why. He'll reveal it." Mrs. Klein replied.

"Ms. Johnson was upset, but when she began to share the turmoil John has been putting her through for the past year, she realized that this may be just the thing God is using to get John's attention. And as bad as it hurts a mother, she said something must give her son an awakening," Mrs. Klein shared with her husband.

"Maybe it's just a father's love that I have. I want the best for all of our students, Deborah," Bishop stresses.

"I know you do. But standing stern as a leader doesn't make you less of a spiritual father. The Bible says to train up a child in the way he should go. So when they grow old, they will not depart from it. Unfortunately, students like John despise that type of teaching. Now is the time to teach him, in his young adult years. By the time he's 40 years old, he'll be a monster, stuck in his old ways. So you've done right. Don't sit here and beat yourself down. Are you coming back in? We're preparing for the meeting."

"I will. Just give me some time with the Lord and I'll be back in shortly." Bishop responded. Mrs. Klein stood to her feet, smiling at her Kenneth.

"Alright. I'm going back in. I'll see you in a moment." Mrs. Klein smiled at him as she departed from his presence.

"Lord, please strengthen me for this meeting. I know the attacks of the enemy are trying to gain force, but he is defeated," Bishop Klein said to the Spirit of the Lord.

"**Look behind you,**" the Spirit of the Lord instructed. Bishop Klein turned around. A woman was laying covered by an old blanket behind a bench near a trash can.

"**The poor will always be among you, my son. Take care of them,**" the Spirit of the Lord said. Bishop stood sadly over the homeless lady. He reached into his wallet, pulled out a hundred dollar bill, and tucked it in between her fingers as she lay on her side. The school bell rang from across the street. Bishop looked over at the school and walked back.

Ruth closed her locker as she walked down the hall, then she stopped.

"I can help you, Evie," Ruth suggested. Evie was struggling to open her locker, the combination on a piece of paper in her hand. Evie grinned stiffly and stood to the side, showing Ruth the combination. Ruth turned the lock, explaining how to use the combination. The locker opened.

"Thank you," Evie grinned. Ruth smiled back.

"I know we have not officially met, but I am Ruth."

"Evie," Evie said stiffly, putting a book into her locker. She shut the door.

"It's good to see you too getting acquainted with one another." Torri walked up to Ruth and Evie. Evie stared at Torri, no longer smiling.

"Yeah, Evie was having some problems with her locker," Ruth smiled, looking at Torri.

"Attention all staff and students, fifth period has been canceled. Please report to the dome immediately. I repeat, all staff and students please report to the dome immediately. All classes for fifth period have been canceled." Students began making their way to the dome.

"Evie, you can walk with us," Torri suggested kindly.

"No, it's okay. I know my way. Thanks Ruth, for helping me with my locker." Evie looked at Torri and walked away. Torri slowly walked down the hall with Ruth, shaking her head with a sigh. Ruth looked at her. They turned the corner. "Here you go with the slow movement again. We really need to get to the other side of the building before the sun goes down," Ruth joked, looking at Torri's serious face. Both ladies continued down the hall.

Students entered the dome noisily. Mrs. Santos, Mrs. Klein, and Bishop were sitting on stage. The large trash bags were to the left of the stage. Mrs. Santos stood up and walked to the microphone.

"Hello everyone, we will get started in just a moment. We are asking that everyone sit on the lower level. Thank you for your cooperation," Mrs. Santos announced. The students moved to the lower level. Evie walked through the auditorium doors and made her way to the third row. She sat down, looking at the stage. The last trickle of students coming through the front door slowed to none. The door closed. Bishop walked to the microphone.

"Good afternoon, students and staff. Many of you are probably wondering why we are here. As you can see, there are five large trash bags on this stage. In them are contraband items we've collected from your lockers. So if there are items missing from your locker today that are against school policy, they are in these bags. If you look to my right and left, you'll see an officer. Many of these possessions we found are not just against school rules but are illegal as well. How they got past security, we're about to find out. This morning, one of your fellow classmates, John Johnson, will no longer be part of this school. After we found a weapon in his locker, he was escorted out by authorities," Bishop shared. Evie looked at Bishop, surprised.

"I and the rest of the administration are very disturbed at what has taken place here. The majority of you are college students that I expected better from. And the things we found in these bags are unacceptable. This school was founded on kingdom principles, and the standards we've set for this school must stand. I refuse to compromise on how God has instructed me to conduct this University," Bishop stressed.

"What sets us apart from every other school in the State of Georgia is our biblical foundation incorporated with our curriculum. For students who have given up during high school, we've added a GED and high school dropout recovery programs so we could motivate and restore hope. Once you complete your high school courses, you can remain at this school for college. But one thing I will not tolerate is disobedient behavior. Now, one of your fellow classmates went to jail this morning, not only because of the gun in his locker but also because he refused to confess the truth. The mercy of God is sufficient to all, but lies benefit no one.

"We have the locker numbers of everyone from whom we confiscated items. The list is here at the front and at the doors. I ask each student who knows that items have been removed from your lockers to come on down to the front. We will deal with each of you appropriately."

"Wow," Evie said to herself and looked around. Torri and Ruth watched her reaction. On the far left of the room, Isaiah sat with his friends. About half of the students were walking toward the front. Mrs. Klein and Mrs. Santos stared at them sternly.

"Quiet down, let me have everyone's attention. All of those who have followed school policies are dismissed, but check the lists on the way out the door, and if your locker number is on the list, please come down with the others. School will begin at its normal time tomorrow. Everyone must clear the premises. I don't want to catch anyone hanging around the school. If any trouble is reported back to me, you may be suspended for up to a week." Bishop instructed. The students began to exit.

"That was right on time. I was just about to whisper to ask you what time it is so I could leave and obey the Lord." Torri told Ruth as they exited the dome. Isaiah spotted Torri on the other side of the room. They made eye contact.

"Call me," Isaiah gestured to Torri, blowing her a kiss. Torri smiled with a blush, nodding her head in agreement. Ruth and Torri walked through the doors. Evie walked far behind them, making her way to the exit doors.

A stocky, light skinned gentleman escorted John into his jail cell. The cell door closed. John looked at his orange jumper down to his feet. He walked over to his cot in distress, shaking his head. The corrections officer turned away and walked down a stairwell.

"Officer Young, please report to cell B48 and bring Yukum to the lounge," the officer on the radio instructed.

"10-4," Young responded. He got on the elevator and pressed three and the doors closed. As he watched the number change from two to three, the elevator jerked to a stop and the double doors opened. The corrections officer got off the elevator, opened up a set of doors, and walked down a hallway. The women in the hall stared at his firm butt and began making comments. He stopped to his left. Two women were in the cell, kissing against the wall. The officer unlocked the cell.

"Okay, you two, step away. Yukum, let's go." Office Young walked into the cell. The two women moved to opposite sides of the cell.

"I'll be back," Yukum told the other woman as the officer cuffed her. They left the cell and Officer Young closed the door securely.

"Kitty will be waiting," the other woman responded. They proceeded down the hall. Women made catcalls and hand gestures as Officer Young escorted Ms. Yukum down the hallway. He opened the steel metal door to access the elevator. Officer Young pressed the button, the doors opened and they entered.

He pressed the B button and the elevator closed. Ms. Yukum looked Officer Young up and down. She made a point of staring at his private area. He watched the elevators reach floor B.

"Man, it looks like you have a horse down there."

"Excuse me?" the Officer responded with a frown. The elevator jerked. She again moved her eyes to his privates, he looked down to where her eyes were viewing. The elevator doors opened.

"Man, let's go." Officer Young grabbed her arm, pulling her along. Tira started laughing contemptuously. They walked down a long hallway and through open doors.

Officer Young turned right and stopped at a desk. Another officer stood up and walked the prisoner into the visitation room.

"Ms. Yukum, you have a visitor." The officer sat her down.

"A visitor?" She asked, peering through the fiber glass.

"Oh, hell, no!" Ms. Yukum picked up the phone receiver.

"Hello, Tira." Torri greeted her cousin.

"What the hell you want?" Tira asked, frowning. Torri sighed, trying not to show the frustration she felt.

"God sent me here," Torri responded.

"Here you go with your superficial God sh.."

Torri interrupted her, "Tira!!! Look, I didn't come here to get into it with you. I came here to see how you're doing. You are my cousin, Tira, and I love you!"

"Save it, Torri. You know I don't like you like that. You always thought you were better than me. Now that I'm in here, you probably really think I'm a…" Tira cusses. Torri rolled her eyes and took a deep breath.

"What's wrong, church girl? My mouth is too filthy for your ears?"

"So have you gone to trial yet?" Torri asked her cousin.

Tira folded her arms. "I'm still on trial," she answered with an attitude.

"Look, this is the time for you to really get right with God. I don't know why you have hardened your heart toward Him. But He is the only answer in this situation. If you are proven guilty for killing all those people, God only knows what's going to happen to you. But I think back to the Bible. Moses was a murderer because he killed an Egyptian for beating a Hebrew man. David was also a murderer. He had another man killed cover the fact that he got his wife pregnant. But with Moses and David, they had hearts of repentance. Even though they paid a penalty for their sin, it wasn't unto death. Tira, are you ready to turn from your wicked ways?" Torri asked.

"No, Torri, I am not! I don't need your God. I told you this before. There is nothing he can do for me that I can't do for myself. You want me to believe in a God who kill babies, that cause disasters in the earth, who make people poor and needy just so someone can call on him for mercy so he can feel powerful? No, thank you! I'll let you be the dummy," Tira replied.

Torri looked at Tira shocked and speechless. **"Torri, your hands are clean, daughter. Say no more. You may leave now and don't look back. Shake the dust off your feet."** The Spirit of the Lord spoke. Torri stood up in shock, silently placed the receiver back on the stand, and walked out.

"Yeah, that's what I thought, church girl," Tira replied arrogantly. She hung up the phone. The officer escorted her back to her cell.

Torri walked out of the visitation room, into a hallway at the window. She signed out, picked up her belongings, and left. The door closed behind her.

"Wow, unbelievable! How can a person harden their hearts to believe there isn't a God? God have mercy on her!" Torri spoke to the Lord as she walked down a hallway.

"Don't pray mercy upon Tira. Pray for My perfect will to be done concerning her." The Spirit of the Lord instructed Torri.

"Praise you, Lord. Let your perfect will be done in this situation, Father, concerning my cousin." Torri got to the top of the hallway. An officer walked past her. Their eyes met.

"Excuse me, do I know you?" The officer stopped and asked Torri.

"I know, you look familiar, too." Torri smiled at him.

"I'm Officer Justin Young." The officer extended his hand. Torri shook his hand, surprised.

"I'm Torri Mansell."

"Torri! Why does your name sound so familiar? My sister and I grew up around a Torri from New York. Torri's face lit up.

"Really! What is your sister's name?" Torri asked him.

Officer Young's radio interrupted. "Officer Young, we need you on block A."

"Okay…be right there," he responded.

"Listen, it was nice to meet you. I have to go." He quickly walked away, leaving Torri speechless.

"Wow, Father! You're doing it like that?" Torri thought as she left the building.

"Be patient, beloved. Evie's process to restoration has already begun." The Spirit of the Lord had Spoken. Torri opened Ruth's car door. She got in and Ruth drove off.

Stay tuned to "The Spirit Has Spoken-His Final Word," Volume No. 3 where Evie's family mystery unfolds.

INVITATION TO SALVATION

Salvation is the most important part of this book. If you've read, "The Spirit Has Spoken," Volume 1, you'll know the battles Evie encountered and how she received salvation. In Volume 2, Evie learned that she must walk out her salvation with fear and trembling. Salvation is a process that doesn't happen overnight. And in order to begin the process, you first must be saved.

Revelation 12:11 reads, **"And they overcame him by the blood of the Lamb and by the word of their testimony, and they did not love their lives to the death."**

Evie's testimony has been given so that you can also be an overcomer by the Blood of the Lamb, who is Jesus Christ. At the end of Volume 1, Evie's testimony of surrendering totally to Jesus Christ was shared to help you make the same decision to follow Him. If you have not done so already, I would like you to pray this first prayer out loud.

FIRST: COME INTO REPENTANCE

1 John 1:8-9 says, [NKJ], **"If we say that we have no sin, we deceive ourselves, and the truth is not in us. If we confess our sins, He is faithful and just to forgive us of our sins and to cleanse us from all unrighteousness."**

"Father, I come before you in the name of Jesus. I repent of all my shortcomings and my sins. I turn away from them and turn to you. I ask you to forgive me for all of the sins I've committed, the sins in my heart and in my thoughts. Thank you, Lord, for your mercy and your grace that endures forever, in Jesus' name, Amen."

Once you have come to Jesus, acknowledging that you have sinned, He can save you. Pray this second prayer with me.

NOW: RECEIVE YOUR SALVATION

Romans 10:9-10 [NKJV] says: **"If you confess with your mouth the Lord Jesus, and believe in your heart that**

God has raised Him from the dead, you will be saved. For with the heart one believes unto righteousness, and with the mouth confession is made unto salvation."

"Father, I believe that Jesus Christ is the Son of God. I believe He died for me, and I ask you to save me now. Dear Lord Jesus, come into my heart, come into my life, and place my feet on the right path - the path of righteousness and the path of serving you. Thank you, Lord Jesus, in Jesus' Name, Amen."

Congratulations! You have made one of the greatest steps of your life by praying those prayers. Now, I encourage you to read your Bible so you can have a clear understanding of what God expects out of your new life walking with Him. I also pray that God sends laborers out on your behalf, leaders of good spirit who will disciple you and raise you up in the things of God. I will continuously keep you in my prayers. God Bless!

PRODUCT

Sequel: Three

ORDER YOUR COPY!

In Sequel Two, "With the mystery that remains, Evie Young still anticipates her parents return with clueless thoughts about their existence. In Sequel Three, she learns to stop fighting against God, after a near to death experience. By obeying The Voice of God, the mystery of her family is solved."

www.ingramcontent.com/pod-product-compliance
Lightning Source LLC
Chambersburg PA
CBHW030515260626
47157CB00005B/1753